TOLL ROAD TO GLORY

By Rusty Welch

Published by:

FriesenPress

Suite 300 – 852 Fort Street
Victoria, BC, Canada V8W 1H8

www.friesenpress.com

Distributed to the trade by The Ingram Book Company

FORWARD

Toll Road to Glory, is a fictional account of the battle of Chickamauga Creek.

The historical events and principal characters that played important roles to shape the events during the three days in the September of 1863 are recorded to history.

The supporting cast that graced that stage in the hills along the Chickamuaga Creek in Northern Georgia has long since been silenced. Their individual stories can no longer be heard, their emotions lost in the undiscovered dimension of time.

Only one's imagination after researching the recorded facts can surmise with some degree of common sense, the wants, fears, and needs of the soldiers laying their lives on the line.

That is why this book is labeled "fiction". Most assuredly only the words from their mouths can be disputed, but not their fundamental spirit of life threatened by no tomorrows on the field of battle.

CHAPTER 1

Major General George Thomas's Chestnut horse struggles to leap up a steep washed-out bank. After several failed attempts the horse finally climbs over the top onto a flat plateau. Thomas reins up his blowing mount and turns to watch his aide, First Sergeant Timothy O'Sullivan's horse stumble over the top, throwing O'Sullivan to the hard dusty surface. Sullivan quickly recovers, and hops to his feet, swearing at the horse. He painfully bends down to pick his kepi up off the ground, slapping the dirt off against his dusty trousers.

General Thomas swings down from his saddle, heartily laughing at the Sergeant, says, "Mr. O'Sullivan, you should consider joining the infantry; you might live a little longer". "Pardon the General Sir, but the General's humor over my misfortune doesn't do anything for the pain. O'Sullivan a giant of a man with paws more fitted for holding tankards, gingerly shuffles to his horse and grabs the reins saying, "If'n the General doesn't mind, I'd like to stay grounded, till I steady me ballast."

Thomas nods, "go ahead Sergeant, but of course you are more entertaining in the saddle".

The view from the plateau offers little militarily. Actually the land is a logistical nightmare, with so many trees. "Braggs Army certainly shouldn't be found in these parts." Thomas mumbles.

Thomas sticks his foot in his stirrup and climbs into the saddle and turns his horse so he can look out to the east. "East", he whispers, stroking his well kept beard, "Bragg, I'll bet that's where you and your ragtag Army lies, just across those low mountains".

Sweat trickles down his face from under his slouch hat. His mind drifts back, remembering the dinner with his Commander, General William S. Rosecran.

I failed to convince Ole Rosie, that Bragg's army is not a defeated army, and far from it. They're just as proud and determined as our Army. Cut from the same cloth. But he just couldn't see it. Well, I've been wrong before, and I Hope I'm wrong this time, only time will tell

"Sergeant, mount up, I've seen all I need too". O'Sullivan, frowns and says, "If the General won't mind, I'll walk the filly down this time". Thomas smiles "Suit yourself Sergeant".

CHAPTER 2

Clouds of dust hang over the valley, as thousands of Union troops march along the dry dusty road, followed by miles of horse drawn wagons stretching as far as the eye can see. Gen. Rosecran's army is on it's way south to find and destroy what's left of Braggs army, somewhere in north Georgia.

General Thomas riding along with Sergeant O'Sullivan in tow, slips in at the head of his XIV Corp. He's still haunted by the decisions made at the dinner with General Rosecran, and is unable to shake off the foreboding feeling he has in his gut.

Rosecran, flushed with victory in Tennessee over Braxton Bragg, is still walking on air.

Bragg has recently vacated Chattanooga, an extremely important transportation hub for the Confederacy, and moved south with his Army, to reorganize after his defeat at Murfreesboro, Tennessee.

A council of war dinner is held by Rosecran with his Corp Commanders at the Carter Hotel in Chattanooga. General Thomas, with his fellow Commanders, General Crittenden, and General Alexander McCook, arrive just as the sun is setting. They are led to a rather large salon on the first floor of the hotel. The room is aglow with lanterns and candles, creating a soft pleasing atmosphere for the Generals, who by now have become accustomed to the rigors and hardships of campaigning.

Cool air circulates through tall Veranda doors, swung open to a small garden. A light breeze causes the candle light reflections to sway and dance across the walls. Sentries, in parade dress, stand guard beside the tall swaying drapes that frame the doors.

A young Corporal, wearing a waiters white waist coat, sets a polished silver tray with glasses, and a selection of liquors on a small table.

General Rosecran pours himself a glass of bourbon, and motions the others to join him.

After the Generals help themselves, Rosecran lifts his glass, to toast, "Atlanta! May we be in Atlanta before the frost flies, gentlemen." He signals for Colonel McKibbon, waiting nearby, to bring the local charts of the area over to a large table and light the two lanterns used to anchor the corners of the maps.

Rosecran unrolls the chart on the table, pauses a moment to take a sip of Bourbon, before dragging his finger down the map, from the Tennessee River in the north, toward the mountains further to the south, and says, "General Thomas, I want you to move the XIV Corp through Stevens Gap, and head east, and proceed on to LaFayette at the other side of Pigeon Mountain.

General McCook, take your XX Corp some twenty miles further south along Lookout Mountain, to Winstons Gap at Alpine.

General Thomas interrupts, "Sir, where's General Crittenden's XXI Corp to be located?"

"Here, a few miles south of Chattanooga, at a place called Rossville. From there he'll move south along the eastside of Missionary Ridge toward Pond Spring.

General Thomas, studies the map, and notices the other Generals facial expressions. Thomas then says, "Your plan Sir, divides our army into three distant parts. Distances that could take a day or two to close if necessary."

"General Thomas, everyday we are picking up Rebel stragglers and deserters. Bragg's Army, is finished. He's falling a part. Disorganized and demoralized. We now have the opportunity to cut the legs out from under the Confederacy, once and for all. The war is all, but over."

Thomas, takes a deep breath, and says, "If you're wrong General, we could lose all we've accomplished this summer".

Rosecran, now visibly annoyed, cuts off the debate, and says, "Generals you have your orders".

The tense atmosphere fills the air, until General McCook breaks the silence with a toast, "To the defeat of Braxton Bragg, once and for all".

A rather strong breeze mysteriously whips through the garden doors, extinguishing many of the candles, as if to suggest a foretelling omen.

CHAPTER 3

General Thomas's Corp halts to take a needed rest, after their long and hot arduous march out of Chattanooga.

The men fall out beside a slow moving creek bordered by large shade trees. A meadow of wild flowers and tall grass that is suitable for the livestock also provides for a soft bedding.

Private John Davis of the 78th Pa., part of General James Negley's Division, lies beneath a tree next to the creek with his buddy, Private James Farr, who's reclining beside him.

"I was just thinking, how much this place reminds me of my swimming hole back home", Farr says. Creeks not quite as wide or deep, but it sure is very similar. Sure wish I was back there now, swimming in that cool water".

"Sounds good, excepting one thing", Davis says.

"Excepting what?"

"Well, if it was my swimming hole, I'd have the prettiest gal in them parts swimming with me, naked of course".

"Damn Davis, Farr says, you done been walking around in my head. That would really be something."

Farr leans up on his elbow to look Davis straight in the face and says "wonder what's that like, you know, to do it in the water?"

Sergeant Bob Drake, resting not far away, quips "it's wetter and a lot cooler than a hot cot in the summertime."

Farr looks over his shoulder at the Sergeant and says, "Sarge, you ever done it in the water before?"

"Nah… whores don't do business in swimming holes son."

Davis burst out laughing, but Private Farr feeling stupid, shrinks back down and pulls his kepi over his eyes.

Private Davis, stares up at a circling Buzzard, and wonders if and when his turn will ever come to experience such things. If ever some girl will ever allow him, Johnny Davis, the chance to explore the frontiers that for now he can only dream of.

CHAPTER 4

General James Negley halts his horse underneath a grove of huge trees and dismounts. He spits a swath of tobacco juice through his heavy mustache, and says, "I don't like it, Colonel".

Colonel Sirwell dismounts, and carefully glances around at the heavily wooded terrain, and says, "Can't say I do either General. Too damn many trees to lay and hide in". Too damn many trees to move an army through, and us a hard days ride, from any meaningful support", Negley adds.

General Negley, pulls a map out of his saddlebag then unties the string wrapped around it and lays the map across his saddle.

He points his finger toward the south and says, "Stevens Gap, and according to this, it should be just up the way. Once we pass through the gap, we'll cross a plain called McLemore's Cove. East of the Cove is Davis Crossroads. There we'll wait for Baird's Division to catch up."

Brig. General Baird's horse slowly plods along the dusty and dung strewn road.

Baird was recently appointed to command the 1st Division, and is ordered to report to General Thomas's HQ.

Weary from his long hot ride, he's uplifted by the sight of the XIV Corp HQ flag, hung beside a shady grove of trees.

1st Sergeant O'Sullivan, on the lookout for Baird, recognizes the General as he leads his horse toward the HQ and shouts out his arrival. Baird rides over to the hitching rope and awkwardly dismounts, stomping his feet a couple of times to get the blood circulating.

General Thomas, with his shirt sleeves rolled up and bare headed steps out of his tent, wearing a broad smile across his face, greets the General with a hearty handshake.

"Sergeant O'Sullivan, Thomas orders, "cut the General a fair portion of beef off the spit, and get him some of that Lemon water you've perfected."

"Yes General Sir, but it will have to be a bit of bacon and biscuits, with black coffee. The beef has spoiled, and the Lemons are gone." "So be it then Sergeant." General Baird, I wish I could offer you better, cause I know it's been a hell of a ride. Come on in and have seat more fitting, for what God intended".

"Thank you General, for your generosity, and care, right now however, anything would be fine, as hungry as I am." Baird says with a light chuckle.

Outside the tent Sergeant O'Sullivan hurries over to the orderly and growls, "mighten you think to secure the Generals horse before it pisses down your boot".

After dressing down the orderly, O'Sullivan notices a Corporal amused by his remarks. He takes only a few strides before he's nose to nose with the Corporal. O'Sullivan's Kepi is pulled down on his face, his chin strap slung tightly under his chin, says "funny is it now. Look at you. Button that blouse, straighten that collar, and clean the dust off yourself ya scab. You are on orderly duty today, not latrine detail, where you will be tomorrow. Now fix yourself." The Corporal jumps back and buttons his tunic.

"When you're done, run over to the cooks tent and get a tin of bacon and biscuits, and a clean cup of coffee, then bring it back here. Mind you, not a drop spilled, nor a thumb print to be found, or you will shovel shit, till you either get kilt or discharged. Now move!" The orderly hops too and runs for the commissary.

"Tis conscripted idiots, they send us". O'Sullivan mumbles.

Baird says, "General, you wouldn't want to transfer that Sergeant to me, by chance? I could sure use a man like that." "Sorry no General, but I've got a couple of young Majors you can have though."

"Now for a different note General, I need you to get your Division through Stevens Gap as quick as you can. General Negley is spread mighty thin, his neck is stuck way out, in country we know nothing about".

Thomas measures the distance on the map and says, " first get some rest, then move out in the morning."

CHAPTER 5

Young Private Judd Archer, a slight lad, who hardly fills out his tattered Butternut uniform, loads canteens onto his packhorse by the bank of the Chickamauga creek.

He's the newest member in his squad that landed him this lonely water detail job, while the rest of his squad is camped on the east side of Pigeon Mountain.

The sun is sinking, casting long eerie shadows across the wilderness.

Judd, yet to prove himself in battle, is still young enough to be influenced by a strong imagination. He is intensely aware of the dangers of a misstep on the rocky path and by the danger from poisonous snakes that could be warming themselves on the stones.

Judd's mind, haunted by these possibilities, walks close beside his only companion the packhorse.

Suddenly, out of the dark, a voice calls out.

"Halt, and identify, or die."

Startled by the unexpected command, Judd drops to a knee. Cold shivers run up and down his spine.

"Identify or die, the strange repeats.

Judd depicts a southern accent this time. His voice shaking, Judd yells, "Private Judd Archer, General Hindman's Division, on water detail."

"I hear ya Archer, so what's the pass word?"

Judd desperately searches through his mind for the password, but nothing, he just can't recall it. He hears a click, the sound a musket hammer makes when cocked.

Suddenly Judd yells at the top of his lungs "Razorback, razorback"!

"Okay, boy you may pass."

Shaken by the ordeal, Judd impatiently coaxes his horse on. As he passes close to a small thicket, he sees the darkened figure of a man hiding in the shadows.

"Boy you came within a squeeze of making your momma a weeping woman." the stranger whispers.

Judd hesitates for a second, before he continues on, slowly leading his horse clopping over the stones.

CHAPTER 6

Cartridge belts and powder horns are slung over stacked muskets, placed around the perimeter of a blazing campfire.

The flickering flames cast an eerie light over the dirty unshaven faces of the men lounging next to the fire.

Popping embers and the nighttime chorus from the insects, provides a sedative for the loneliest of hearts in the evening chill.

A faint unnatural sound, filters into the camp from way off in the dark.

All eyes around the campfire strain to focus in the dark to determine what the disturbance could be.

Out from the dark, Judd steps leading his laden packhorse.

"Well, look who we have here. It's damn sure about time boy," cracks Zach Sanger, a scruffy looking character not much older than Judd, but hardened and battle tested. "Figured you done and lit out for home to hide behind your momma's skirts."

"That creek ain't just over the hill you know." Judd shouts back. "Besides, I pert near got myself shot by a damn picket of ours, getn this here water."

"Hell, Judd boy, you done good fetchen the water, but where's supper, I don't see no damn deer slung over that beast." cackles Bay Thompson. "Yea, what we suppose to eat, uh?" Laughs Chick Hartley. "You best be a getn back out there and rustle us some possum or squirrel. You know, you young fellers suppose to take care of us older battle hardened veterans, by God."

Judd not amused, begins unloading the horse, scattering the canteens over the ground. He then says "Chick, hope next time, Sergeant Sawyer, sends you after the water, for sure."

"Yea Sergeant, send Chick, I can smell possum frying in the pan now." Bay cackles.

Zach, searches through the scattered canteens looking for his initials, "Z.S." burnt into the side, says above the laughter, "Bay there ain't gonna be no smell of possum in your nostrils boy, causen you're gonna smell the stench of blue bellies rotten in the sun real soon."

"How's that be Zach Sanger, you got gyspy cards in them tattered pockets of yourns?" Chick said.

Zach finally finds his canteen and brushes the dirt off then says, "I can sniff a battle days and days before it actually happens, and we damn sure got one coming, mark my words".

Pa Jones, a huge man, as big as a tree, and older than the rest, lifts his fry pan off some heated rocks to examine his biscuit sizzling in the fat.

Bay Flounders, standing next to Jones, tosses a log on the fire causing sparks and ash to shoot out of the fire. Pa, leaps back trying to protect his pan with his other hand, and hollers "Bay you are as dumb a boy as I ever did see. You ever do that again and I'll take a strap and wup you good, you here?"

Bay, falls backwards loudly laughing at the aspect of getting walloped, says "Old man you best be saving some of that energy for them there yanks, Zach says is coming." "Never mind about my energy, I hope them Yanks are coming this way, and the sooner the better." Pa quips.

Pa squats back down by the fire, and sets his pan back on the heated rocks.

Judd asks "Why is it you be wanten them yanks to be a coming for?"

"Cause, young feller, I'm itchen to get me a pair of them britches they wear, and a pair of brogans that ain't leaken. Maybe get me some real coffee them Yanks got too."

Sergeant Sawyer walks up to the fire and orders "Ya'll, boil your water before turnen in, I don't wanna see nobody droppen out cause ya got the shits."

"They ain't never nobody done boiled no water for them horses there. And they ain't shitten no more than normal." Bay said.

"You know Bay, the Lord takes care of dumb animals, so I guess Bay you don't have to boil your water. The rest of ya take heed of what I said."

"Bay how'd you ever learn to drink from a cup, and eat with a fork?" jest Zach.

"Never you mind, Zach Sanger, never you mind, or I'll lay this here log across yore head." Bay threatens.

Judd sits down next to Pa, and asks, "That part about robben the dead, ain't that same as murderen for money?"

Pa sticks his fork in his biscuit and says "Nah, not in this here war, son. You stay around a while and you'll be a outfitten yourself too boy. Or go naked."

Judd glances at the soles of his shoes and then quietly stares at the dancing flames.

Pa, stands up, pats Judd on the head, and says "Judd, don't knows why I'd join an Army so poor, but I done and did like some fool. A mans got needs, from time to time."

CHAPTER 7

Major General Braxton Bragg, a man hated by most, and in command of many. Put in charge of the Army of Tennessee, by President Jeff Davis, himself. Both were classmates at West Point, in the 40's, and both are committed to secure independence for the South.

Bragg, a demanding narcissist, is blessed with a face akin to that of a Neanderthal.

It's now near evening, as the sun begins to sink behind Pigeon Mountain.

Bragg stomps back and forth in front of a huge campfire blazing in front of the farmhouse he uses for his Head quarters.

Chomping on the stub of a worn out cigar, he curses under his breath. Several uneasy staff officers wait nervously by, taking care to stay out of his way.

"Where the hell, is that damn scout?" he snaps.

Is he working for me or Rosecran?"

One of the staff officers sheepishly responds, "Does the General want to send out a patrol to find him?"

"In the dark?" Bragg responds.

"Send out some couriers and find out if General Polk or Hill have heard anything on the where a bouts of Rosecran's Army."

"That won't be necessary General," a man says as he rides in out of the dark, and dismounts. The stranger spits in the fire, "sorry I'm late. Your picket line is diligently doing their duty."

Bragg not amused, says, "They're the only ones."

"Well now General, as you know it's a fair piece from Winston's Gap. Been doen some real hard riden, and could sure use a morsel or so to eat."

"Tell me where the hell Rosecran is then you can eat till you drop." Bragg impatiently announces.

"Yes, well General the Yanks are definitely on their way. But strangely they have done and split themselves up.

They got the XX Corp clear down at Winston's and the XIV up at Stevens Gap, and the XXI up near Rossville. Each one is some twenty miles apart. Hell you can knock them off one at a time like bottles shot off a dang fence."

Bragg's face relaxes for the first time that night. He tosses his spent cigar into the fire, and says, "Rosecran, thinks we're finished. Well… I'll show him who is finished, and who isn't. Sir, you've earned your food this day, Major get this man all he wants to eat."

Bragg spins around on his heels and hurries into his Head quarters, yelling back, "Someone find a couple of couriers, with fast horses."

CHAPTER 8

General Thomas Hindman, younger than most of his officers, is a handsome looking man in his early thirties. He looks more like an up-start than a Division commander. Wise beyond his years, this Mexican war Veteran, has earned the respect of his superiors and his subordinates, as well.

General Hindman steps down off his horse, and ties it to a tree. He unbuckles his saber belt, hanging it over his saddle horn. A corporal comes running over and apologies for not handling his horse when he arrived.

"Corporal, stand down, I can handle him fine."

"Yes Sir, General, step this way for General Polk."

In amongst the trees lies a primitive cabin, with two large flat stones providing the only steps up to a small open porch.

Hindman, tries to brush the dust off his coat and trousers on his way to the cabin.

General Polk steps out of the door on to the porch. The sometime Episcopal Bishop, presently a Corp commander, welcomes General Hindman, "the comforts aren't much, I'm afraid. Times have been better, as you know."

They shake hands, and enter the cabin. "The inside is as austere as the outside, as you can see." Pope apologizes.

The inside is dim and feels damp, with a musty odor. In the far corner is a small fireplace. A small table in the center of the room provides the only furniture besides a cot against a wall. An oil lantern on the table provides the only light for his map of the area.

"When I look at the depressing conditions here in the cabin, I quickly remember the conditions our Lord suffered under." Polk mentions. "Amen". Hindman adds.

"Now General, to get to the business at hand, our honorable leader General Bragg, has ordered your Division to march south and engage the enemy at McLemore's cove.

Rosecran is expected to use the gap, called Steven to move one of his Corps east."

"How is my one Division, going to stop a whole federal Corp?" Hindman ask.

"That's the blessing. He's split his Corps into three parts. If we can catch them as they enter the Cove with their leading Division, we will have a two to one advantage."

"You say two. Where is the other Division?"

"General Cleburne, will attack from the east at the same time you attack from the north."

General Polk, circles the place on the map.

"General Polk, coordinating the attack between our Divisions, will be paramount. We'll need to communicate some how or establish a time table of sort."

"Yes, of course. Try and be on the field by six o'clock, before sun up. You'll need to lay low, so as not to be seen. You'll have to judge that, depending on the terrain.

Cleburne's artillery will open fire, when his skirmish line makes contact with the enemy. When you hear his cannons, start your attack. Your objective is to destroy the Yankee Division before it crosses the cove. With that accomplished, don't stick around. Get back to friendly ground."

Hindman drags his finger along the map and says "This road, what kind condition is it in?"

"Primitive, wagon rut most of the way, unfortunately."

"I see. General I should get the Division started on the road by midnight I think. So…"

General Polk interrupts, "So, good luck, and may God be with you."

CHAPTER 9

Some ten miles south of Polks HQ, is D. H. Hill'S Corp Headquarters on the eastern slope of Pigeon Mountain.

General Hill is another one of those difficult, narrow minded, self admiring, southern Generals, transferred out of Lee's Army, because of his attitude. His new assignment with Bragg hasn't changed him one bit.

Bragg's courier stands at attention in front of General Hill, while the General reads Bragg's directive. His face reddens, as he slowly crumples up the paper. He abruptly jumps to his feet, shoving his folding chair back over the makeshift wooden floor, and dismisses the Lieutenant waiting in front of him.

The Lieutenant feeling the heat, snaps a salute and hurries away.

Hill, stomps out of the building, on the lieutenant's heels, and tosses the crumpled order into the campfire.

Hill's insubordinate behavior does not go unnoticed by his junior officers warming by the fire.

Hill growls, "If that Ape thinks he can squander away one of my Divisions with some lunatic notion, that Rosecran will come looking for us with only one Division, he's lost his mind. "He'll shovel shit first." Hill, reaches down picks up a log and slings it in the fire. Still fuming, he says, "Bragg can waste Buckner's men, but he ain't killing mine, with some idiotic plan. He shouldn't be allowed to wear the chevrons of stable boy."

General Bragg, insuring his order is carried out, sent a copy of the directive to General Cleburne, knowing Hill's reputation.

General Cleburne steps into the firelight, ties up his horse and is dismayed when he hears the ranting and raving Hill is spewing in front of the men standing around the fire.

Almost speechless, Cleburne manages to say, "General Hill Sir, may I see you privately in your headquarters."

"General Cleburne, Hill replies, tilting his head to the side, let me guess, why you have graced us with your presence."

"General, I have orders here from General Bragg, we need to discuss."

"No need to Sir, I have already taken care of that." Hill gestures toward the fire.

"General, you can't ignore, General Bragg's order." Cleburne pleads. "That's a courts martial offense, General."

"Not if it is found to be illogical, and illegal." Hill counters. "Besides you're too ill to lead the attack."

Cleburne, flabbergasted at this bold face lie, loudly protest, "General Hill…" Hill, not willing to debate the issue, interrupts Cleburne, "A courts martial, Sir, that would be a most welcomed event. Expose that Ape's stupidity and run the lunatic out of this Army. Hell, maybe he'll switch sides."

Cleburne stunned by this latest outburst says, "Our conversation should continue in your headquarters."

Hill's eyes narrow as he studies the expression on Cleburne's face. His lips tighten. "Yes, General Cleburne, I'll see you in my Headquarters."

Hill turns and stomps through the tent door with Cleburne fast on his heels.

Once inside Hill produces two tin cups and a bottle of bourbon. He pours and fills the cups to the top, hands Cleburne one and lifts his cup to toast and says "To your recovery". Cleburne is reluctant to join him, but takes a small sip. Hill ignores the slight and begins to speak with a calmer tone. "General Cleburne, you and General Hindman have been directed to coordinate an attack against the Federals that Bragg believes is stupid enough to bring only one Division to the field. Not hardly.

The road you are to use will take hours and hours of hard labor to make it passable for your artillery. That, in itself demonstrates there isn't the time. Secondly it's suicidal to have two small Divisions risk life and limb, and then retreat. That's stupendously stupid, and that's why you aren't going."

General Cleburne, set his cup down when Hill finishes, and softly says "every thing you said sounds truly logical, except for one thing."

Cleburne takes a sip of his Bourbon.

"General you're a soldier, and you expect your orders to be followed without exception, and General Bragg, expects the same from you."

"General, I will move my men out as ordered.

Hill's face turns beet red, and loudly threatens "I forbid you to move one platoon from this Corp Sir! Not one squad, you hear!"

Cleburne tugs his hat down over one eye, and replies, "I have my orders from higher up… so court martial me if you wish."

CHAPTER 10

Private Johnny Davis and James Farr are sound asleep in their cramped tent, recovering from the days rigorous march. All is dark and peaceful, excepting the chorus of snores escaping the canvas enclosures.

Suddenly a harsh racket shatters the still of night. The pounding of hundreds of horses hoofs, and clanging harnesses as cavalry troops, with caissons, and artillery pieces race down the lane between the bivouac shelters.

Sergeant James Drake hurries along the tents barking orders "shake it out, toss and roll them blankets, grab your socks. Get out of them sacks, piss and crap, and get breakfast. Move it, shake it out. Nobody falls out today, there will be no stragglers today."

Drake repeats the same thing over and over as he makes his way down the row of tents.

Farr sticks his head out of his tent just as Sgt. Drake passes by. Drake looks down at Farr and spits "you deaf or dumb boy, get your ass moving. Get breakfast, crap in the hole, and fall in."

Jumping up, Farr quickly rolls his blanket, and unbuttons his tent half, rolling it over his blanket. Davis, moving slower, urges Farr to go get breakfast without him. "I'll catch up James, you go on ahead."

A couple hundred yards up the road, General Negley, sits on his cot half dressed, pulling up his knee high boots.

His aide sticks his head in the tent and says "Good morning General."

"It's a little early to conclude Major, if it's a good morning or not."

"What would the General like for breakfast this morning?"

"Same as the men, Major."

"Biscuits, General?"

"Biscuits, Major."

Negley stomps his feet on the ground and pulls up his suspenders. Gets his coat on and takes a cigar from the pocket, and leans over an oil lantern puffing to get it lit. His first sergeant arrives with a pot of coffee and says "The men are forming up, and men are standing by outside to strike your tent when you're ready Sir."

"Thank you Sergeant."

Negley accepts the cup of coffee from Sgt. Bradshaw, and hands him his saber, "put this on my saddle please."

Back down the hill from the General's quarters, Sgt. Drake is busy getting his men lined up. "You bunch of worm dung, line it up, come on, two rows, this ain't your first formation, dress it right, let's go.

Private Long runs down the wooded hill, buttoning his pants without missing a step. He dashes around the front row and jumps in next to Johnny Davis, forcing the others to move down, to make room.

Sergeant Drake steps in front of Private long and whispers, "Mr. Long are you an officer, Mr. Long?" Long with a puzzled look on his face, meekly answers "No Sergeant, not that I'm aware of." Drake continues politely, "then, why tell, isn't your blouse buttoned?" His voice grows louder and harsher, " button that blouse, while you still have buttons to button." Noticing the amused expression on Private Davis's face, Sergeant Drake turns to him, and says, "Private Davis, do I look funny to you this morning?" Davis shakes his head no.

"The funny thing Private Davis is, you and your friend Long, will have plenty to laugh about together tonight digging crap holes, provided of course you both are still alive tonight. Now square this line and dress right," he shouts.

Lt. Simeon, standing off to the side, watches Sgt. Drake form up the men. He steps forward, takes a deep breath as he musters up a commanding voice and announces, "Today we may encounter the enemy. I know you will all do you duty. We will be crossing a creek, how deep I don't know, so take care to keep your powder dry. We are deep in enemy territory, so no straggling. If you need to go, hold it till we break. Sgt. Drake you can move the men out."

CHAPTER 11

In the chilly darkness, a ghostly gray clad line of men shuffle down a wagon trail, beside the foggy Chickamauga Creek. The orchestra sounding music from the crickets and frogs chirping, mixed with the muffled sound of marching feet, provides a peaceful rhythm.

Bay Flounders, marching behind Zach Sanger says, "Zach, you damn sure got the nose alright, sniffing out this here battle." "Sure enough Bay, and the smell is getting powerful strong," Zach responds.

Chick Hartley says, "Pa, if'n I get a shot at one of them bigger ones, I'll be a let'n you know." Pa looks over his shoulder at Chick and says, " Chick you chop em down, and I'll skin em down, son."

"Yea, but ya gotta share their coffee." Chick adds.

Sergeant Sawyer marching at the front yells back "and I hope the big Yank craps in his britches, when he croaks." Pa hollers back, "Sergeant, Yankee dead don't shit, they just swell and pop there dang buttons."

Lt. Bishop riding along side the platoon hearing the chatter quips "Private Jones, not to worry, I've instructed our artillery to aim high, to save them trousers for ya."

Bay Flounders asks, "How's shooten high gonna kill any Yanks?" "Bay you'd be dumber than a rabid coon biting its own tail." quips Zack. "I'm dumb, hell, I heard yore family once, up and bought a three legged mule. Ya wanna share that story with us huh Zach?"

"Sure do. We saved the things life from this poor family, getting ready to eat another one of the damn things legs. Their family name was Flounders I heard."

"Zack, you done messed where you shouldn't boy. When we be stoppen, I'm gonna make certain you'll be gummin your next supper, you hear."

"That's enough now, ya'll save your animosity for the Yanks," Lt. Bishop scolds.

A short while later, Bay taps Judd on the shoulder and whispers, "What's that animosity thing mean?"

"It's something to eat Bay," he says.

"Why would we wanta save our grub for them there Yanks, huh?"

"Causen, we gonna kill them with kindness Bay." Zack answers.

The dark eastern sky pales as morning approaches, silhouetting the mountaintops, against the pink horizon. The birth of a new day brings sweet music to the ears, echoing out of the dense forest from the birds, replacing the sound of tired crickets. The soothing symphony eases the troubled minds of the men marching towards the unknown.

Ten miles to the south, axes ring out as men hurry to clear the way through Dug's Gap on Pigeon Mountain.

General Cleburne sits on his horse, weary after a night of pushing his men to clear a path for his batteries to pass over.

CHAPTER 11

Col. Sirwell leads his regiment through the pass on Missionary Ridge to the banks of the Chickamuaga Creek, halting to check for Confederate skirmishers.

Col Sirwell dismounts, to inspect the integrity of the ground along the creek bank where he intends to cross. "Sergeant, have the men dismount and rest the horses."

The Colonel has most of his brigade on escort duty with the supply wagon train, leaving him perilously weakened.

He feels extremely uneasy, with only a hundred men this far deep in enemy territory. Surely there has to be Confederate spies watching his every move.

Captain Miller dismounts and walks with his horse in tow, to meet with the Colonel by the creek, to discuss their next move.

"Joe, I think the best ground appears to be over there, where we'll try and cross the creek. I'll test the depth first, before we get started. When we do get in have the men water their horses. After that, I want to send out a six man patrol by pairs, in three directions. Have them report back to me in four hours." "Yes Sir", Miller said.

Colonel Sirwell leads his horse on foot over to the crossing and down to the waters edge, carefully looking for any sign of trouble. Once at the water, he climbs up into his saddle and nudges the horse forward, wading out into the middle of the creek. All is well. He scans the plain of McLemore Cove on the other side. No sign of any enemy activity. Sirwell waves the men forward to join him in the creek.

Captain Miller splashes down into the creek and rides up along side Sirwell.

"Well Captain, the ground across the creek appears to be dry. Go ahead and send the scouts out. We'll proceed as planned," orders Sirwell.

"Yes Sir."

"Lt. Deedham, scouts out, then form up the troop by twos." Captain Miller shouts.

The men stream out of the creek with Colonel Sirwell in the lead.

CHAPTER 12

Gen. Hindman, sits resting in his saddle on a hill above McLemore Cove, watching his Division form up on the rolling ground below. He lights a cigar and watches the smoke drift towards the north. It is 06:30.

A courier rides out of the brush behind him. His horse is bathed in sweat. The courier gasping for air says, "General I have an urgent message for you Sir."

Hindham, turns in his saddle and takes the message, and says, "You trying to kill that horse Corporal?" "No Sir, I was told to waste not a minute Sir."

"I see." Hindman opens the message from General Polk.

It reads "General, imperative, as soon as you conclude your mission there, hurry back. The Federal 21st Corp is on the move south from Rossville."

Hindman, looks at the courier, and can tell he is in no condition to ride back.

"Major, send another courier to General Polk, and inform him, we are on the field, and waiting for General Cleyburne's arrival. Understand the urgency of the situation. Get that out quickly," Hindham orders.

Soon after, another courier arrives with a message from General Cleyburne, informing he is late deploying his skirmish line due to conditions in the mountain pass, and adds, " May take several more hours, will inform when ready."

This information puts General Hindman in a sticky spot. Should he continue with the mission, or hurry back to Polk? The element of surprise could easily become compromised by this delay.

He climbs down out of his saddle asking for his field glass.

Nervously, adjusting the focus, to scan over the misty field below him. Back and forth he sweeps the glass. Suddenly, off in the far distance he notices two specks approaching from the south. At first he can't determine their identity, until they get closer and become clearer. He can now see they are Union cavalry soldiers, obviously on a scouting mission.

Surely his skirmish line will hold their, fire until the riders can safely be captured or killed, he thinks to himself.

Suddenly eight riders in his cavalry gallop out firing as they chase after the strangers.

"Damn it all to hell! Hindman shouts. Major, ride down there and find out who is responsible for sending out that pursuit party, and then relieve the son of a bitch of his duties."

Hindman notices one of the Union troopers tumble from his saddle in a cloud of dust. The other rider bent down low in his saddle gains distance on his pursuers. "Damn, he's going to get away," Hindman whispers. The stranger slowly disappears out of sight.

Hindman lowers his glass. "That scout, he thinks to himself, has enough information to compromise the whole damn plan."

He sticks a cigar in his mouth, and rides back to join his staff. "Major, send a courier to General Cheatham, and inform him our presence has been compromised, and that I wish to confer with him. I will ride and meet him half way."

CHAPTER 13

General Negley and his Division has been on the road since dawn. The men, marching all day in the grueling hot sun, are too tired to celebrate when they stop for the night across the east side of the Chickamauga Creek.

Col. Sirwell a few miles further east had halted an hour earlier, to let the Division close up some, and also get his skirmish line set up to warn them if the enemy appears.

Back at the Divisions camp, the men wasted little time, dumping their packs and collapsing on the ground.

Cook squads get busy, starting cook fires and raising serving tents.

The men are a soar sight; covered from head to toe in dried red dirt from the dust that settled after they had waded out of the creek.

Sergeant Drake walks up to a small clearing where he finds his weary ward sprawled out across the ground. "Private Long, Private Davis, off your butts. You two jesters have shit trenches to dig, because we have a whole Division full of crap, so let's move it!" he says menacingly.

"Sergeant, I've got nothing left," Davis pleads

"You, and Private Long will report to the Quartermaster, and draw picks and shovels, right now."

General Negley sitting on a campstool reads over his map, as several soldiers labor to raise his headquarter tent.

Colonel Sirwell weaves his horse around and through the busy soldiers setting up the camp, looking for General Negley.

Major Felig sees him and hollers, "Colonel Sirwell, over here." Sirwell hastens over and dismounts, shaking hands with Major Felig, and handing his horse to an orderly.

"The General will be glad to hear from you, he's kind of been a bit anxious today." Felig said.

"Yes, and I fear he may soon have good reason." Sirwell, tells Felig, as they hurry to meet the General.

General Negley cordially offers his hand instead of the customary salute. "Colonel, I am so glad to see you."

Thank you General, I certainly wish I could offer better news I'm afraid."

Negley's friendly expression quickly evaporates, and ask "Colonel, what is it you've found out?"

"Well General, I sent scouts out to the north, south, and east this morning. The south scout reported nothing of consequence, but the east pair heard a great deal of noise, sounding like the cutting of timber. My northern pair ran into a sizable enemy formation. Only one managed to get back."

"So, it sniffs of a two pronged attack maybe."

"Could be, and the force to the north is not far from here, and I have to believe they would'nt send an under-manned force to contest our arrival. In all probability they already know our strength," Sirwell says.

General Negley, stares at Sirwell for a moment, pondering the issue, and then says, "I have only four regiments and a mounted company on hand. My nearest supporting element, is General Baird's brigade, and he is still some ten miles further back."

"Colonel, I am going to pull back to Stevens Gap. You will cover us as best you can, while pulling back yourself. Have your artillery pieces move with us. I'll meet with you in the Gap. Good luck Colonel.

"Major tell the officers to prepare to break camp and move out immediately and recall our pickets," Negley orders.

Felig pauses a second, and says, "you know I'd sure hate to be in a Sergeant's shoes, around here right now."

A ways out from the main camp, Privates Davis and Long, sit exhausted atop a pile of dirt, sweating, bare chested, staring into the ditch they have struggled to excavate. "You know something Davis, the one good thing about all of this, is that we'll each have our own tents to sleep in tonight." Long casually mentions. "Yea, how about that, that's right, with the other boys, sent out on picket duty. I wonder if Sergeant Drake figured that out yet." Davis laughs.

Generals Cheatham and Hindman, meet on the road, their brigade colors held by the color guards atop tall staffs, is reminiscent of the knights of old. Cheatham doffs his plumed hat to Hindman as he greets him, and says "General, I am at your service Sir." "Thank you General Cheatham, I anticipate you have arrived at an opinion about rather to continue this mission."

"General, if I viewed this through the eyes of our enemy, provided of course your presence was detected, he would do whatever he could to avoid contact until he was able to grow his numbers appreciably."

"Well put. I of course have General Cleyburne, to consider. I feel I have to be available to support his effort and think to contact him would be prudent. So, I am releasing you from your obligation to support me so you may return to your duties with General Polk."

"General Hindman, I will take the necessary steps to get back to General Polk and inform him of our talk." General Cheatham politely tips his hat and rides away with his staff.

Hindman sends a courier to advise Cleyburne of the situation, and that he would wait for word from him.

CHAPTER 14

Darkened figures of stooped Union troops plod along in the black of night.

Private Davis, his heavy musket hung over his sagging shoulder complains to Private long, marching ahead, "Peaceful night, a tent of our own, huh." Long replies, "Davis war isn't all brass bands and bugles is it."

The opportunity to pounce on the unsuspecting Union division had been lost. The ghost, had up and fled in the dark of night.

As luck would have it, Bragg's bad deal was turning up aces. His Army is growing with reinforcements from all over the south. General Longstreet with his Division is on his way from Virginia, on loan from Lee. General John B. Hood, still recovering from injuries suffered at Gettysburg, is leading his Corp to join Bragg.

The men in Hindman's Division march over the familiar road they tramped the night before. Bay Flounders, decides it is time to stir the pot a little. "Hey Zach, where's them there Blue Bellies, you was a sniff'n?"

"Never you mind Bay, you'll be a gettin your fill soon enough. My nose ain't never let me down yet."

Young Judd Archer, feeling more accepted by his comrades, says "I sure hope something happens soon, my feet done wore out." "Judd you'd best be advised to take care of what you wishin for, causen it ain't gonna be no picnic, when we run em down." Zach counters. "Amen" Pa Jones adds.

CHAPTER 15

General Thomas Crittenden, with his XXI Corp moves south toward Ringgold, east of the Chickamauga Creek. Crittenden wants to move slowly, probing his front for any sign of Rebel activity. He sends his celebrated tough little General, Thomas Woods ahead with his 1st Division. Wood a slight man, looks more like a European Prince. He is highly regarded by his superiors, as well as the men in his command. General Sherman once made the remark "he was worth two thousand men in a scrap."

Marching through the tangled woods, to shield his presence, General Wood plans to stop and wait at a place called Lee and Gordon's Mill. He has no idea he is marching right through the shadow of General Polk's Corp.

Bragg's second opportunity in as many days is offered up on a platter. The crumbs are falling right in his lap.

More reinforcements have arrived by now, including Generals Breckinridge, Bushrod Johnson, Simon Buckner, and William Walker. Bragg's ranks swelling to a numerical advantage over the boys in Blue.

All is quiet across the Georgian Front, except in General Rosecran's HQ. Disturbing reports of enemy activity are received from General McCook to the south and General Negley's close call at McLemore Cove.

Bragg attempts to seize upon another opportunity to knock off an isolated portion of Rosecran's Army. He pens an order to mobilize General Polk's Corp. Have Polk cross the Chickamuaga Creek north of Lee and Gordon's Mill and sweep south, he will out match the Union Division waiting for Crittenden at Lee & Gordon's Mill. The plan is brilliant, if all the units coordinate on time, roll south in order, and smother the Union's inferior force before it can be reinforced. The Domino plan begins with General Bedford Forrest's cavalry and infantry to begin the initial strike.

Rosecran slowly wakes up and smells a rat. He confers with his Chief of staff General James A. Garfield to get his thoughts on what he thinks might be pending.

"I'm of the opinion that the thing General Thomas feared most about our strategy is exactly on the money."

Rosecran, sensitive to criticism, never the less, has to face the truth. He quietly examines the map with red circles indicating the reported enemy locations.

Garfield lays his glasses down on the map and says "General I would advise you to waste no more time and order Crittenden, and McCook to move at once to consolidate with Thomas. Meet in the middle so to speak."

Rosecran fidgets with his pen, puffs on his cigar then asks, "If we consolidate to far south, our supply lines in and around Chattanooga are vulnerable. If Bragg swings north we will have to fight our way out."

"You have General Grangers reserve Corp to punish any effort made toward Chattanooga." General Garfield says.

Rosecran finally saya, "Colonel McKibbon, execute orders for Generals Crittenden and McCook to strike out at once and move to join up with the XIV Corp's respective flanks north of Stevens Gap.

General Garfield, continues studying the map, and makes special notice of possible crossings over the Cickamuaga Creek, and says "I would strongly suggest, these crossings north of Lee and Gordon's Mill be defended, while General Crittenden marches south to protect his rear."

"Mounted troops, would best accomplish that at this time. Need to find out who is closest, and issue the necessary order. "Well, I feel better about things now." Rosecran sighs.

Garfield stuffs his glasses in his pocket and says, "hopefully General time is on our side."

CHAPTER 16

Colonel Minty rides quietly along the dark LaFayette road in the early hours before dawn.

On his mind, is how best to defend the Reed's Bridge with his cavalry brigade, if it becomes necessary.

He arrives at the bridge as the sun's first rays paint the eastern sky. A low mist floats over the waters of the Chickamuaga Creek. Minty nudges his horse forward onto the bridge. The clatter of the horse's hooves on the wood planking is amplified in the still morning air. He waits on the east side of the creek for his aide, Major Potter to catch up. "Major tell the men to water their horses, while I check out that ridge in front of us."

Minty spurs his horse to a gallop, and takes off for the ridge.

The cool morning air makes it easier for his horse to climb the rising ground leading to Pea Valley Ridge. The view from the top of the ridge offers a good position to command the ground in front for some distance. Minty dismounts and pours some oats into his hat and feeds his horse. He looks around, then mounts back up and rides back to the bridge.

"Major, the ground on the Ridge has good defensive qualities. We'll set up there. I want you to take a company and reconnoiter Leets Tanyard on the other side of Pea Valley Creek. I need to know if they've got a Rebel contingent over that way."

Major Potter, halts his company behind a cornfield, and has them dismount. Leaving Lt. Giles, his second in command to wait with the Company, Potter takes Sgt. Fennigan and ten other men to check out Pea Valley Creek.

They creep along the ground through the cornfield, and up to the far end of the field. Potter focuses his binoculars on a small mill beside the creek. "Sergeant take a couple of men with you, and check that mill out."

Potter watches Fennigan sneak towards the mill. He reaches the back wall and peers around the corner. He motions for one of the men with him to look through the door and check inside the building.

The soldier slowly pushes the door open, and steps inside, where he comes face to face with a scruffy looking character in a filthy gray waist jacket. The startled stranger reacts as if he'd bumped into a ghost.

The scruffy stranger drops his musket, and falls backwards over a bucket, causing the bucket to roll into a cogwheel jamming the wheel.

The startled Rebel screams "Yankees, Yankees," as he tries to scramble to his feet.

The frightened Union soldier, stumbles back out the door, and trips over a step, falling to the ground.

Sergeant Fennigan runs over to try and help the hapless soldier, when shots ring out from across the creek. He jumps back behind the wall, to take cover. The unfortunate soldier lying on the ground reaches for his musket and attempts to scoot on his knees to reach the safety of the wall, when a ball slices through his neck, sending him sprawling to the ground, choking and drowning in his own blood from the massive wound.

Fennigan, leans out around the corner to see several Rebels leap into the creek and labor to wade through the water.

Fennigan takes aim and fires at one of the pursuers, who jerks around and falls backwards into the water.

The other two Union soldiers open fire on the Rebs crossing in the creek, giving Fennigan enough cover to escape from the building. He runs away from the building, and orders everyone to follow.

The scampering men reach the edge of the cornfield and slide down hard, beside Major Potter. Fennigan panting heavily gasp, "Major, them rebels are fired up and coming as mad as hell. Private Bradley caught one in the throat, he wont be coming." "I guess we best get the hell out of here then." Potter yells.

They jump up and race through the cornfield, yelling for the other men waiting with the horses, to mount up and ride for the ridge.

Major Potter and his men ride like the wind to get back to Pea Valley Ridge, to warn Colonel Minty of the pending threat.

The Southern troops at the Mill are a part of Bushrod Johnson's Division, camped along side General Bedford Forrest's Cavalry troopers.

The brief action at the Mill has gotten the attention of Forrest who is well known for his hot temper and unbounded bravado.

Johnson orders the bugler to recall the soldiers that were in pursuit. Knowing damn well, that it was only a small reconnaissance party they were chasing. What concerns him is the reason behind the patrol, and how many Federals are in his sector. A proper plan of action can only be prepared when understanding what the enemy's intentions might be. Are they defensive or offensive in nature?

General Forrest rides up with a small staff, and joins, General Johnson on the edge of the creek, by the Mill.

The Cavalier Forrest, wearing his plumed hat, is the epitome of Southern breeding.

"General Johnson, I missed the skirmish, did we harvest any prisoners Sir?"

"No General, the creek impeded our chase, I'm afraid. I will set up a proper pursuit, when my scouts return. Right now I have no idea where they came from, and why."

"Well General, I will tell you."

General Johnson, feeling a bit slighted, by the tone in Forrest's commit, curtly says "Sir, pray tell where might they be, and why?" General Forrest removes his hat and points with it toward the west. "There, where Reed's Bridge crosses the Chickamuaga. They probably have a brigade or possibly a Division defending it. It's quite logical they would want to protect their left flank by controlling that bridge."

Forrest puts his hat back on and says "Be it coincidental, or not, but I just received a communiqué from Braxton, ordering us to cross that bridge with the Division, and begin to attack south. I am waiting for the rest of my troopers to return from their reconnaisance to commence the operation."

Johnson, angrily protests, "I have received no such word of this, from General Bragg."

Forrest curtly hands him the directive and says, I am delivering it now, as you will read, this operation will be under my Command."

Johnson reads the message, the expression on his face changes to one of disbelief. He slowly hands it back to Forrest, and says nothing.

"Now General, alert the Division to be ready to move out at the earliest possible moment. Inform your officers, to expect resistance near the Pea Valley Ridge. My mounted infantry will join you there."

CHAPTER 17

Colonel Minty, prepares his defensive line along the Ridge, and sends out a picket line. He also places half of his command closer to the bridge itself, aided by his artillery. The possibility of the Confederates overwhelming the ridge, hasn't escaped his mind. He may be forced to implement a fighting retreat and doesn't want to worry about abandoning his cannon. Minty doesn't have to worry about his southern flank since Colonel Wilder and his Lightning Brigade are defending the Alexander Bridge.

General Johnson rides cross the Pea Vine Creek, the men in his Division follow, gingerly wading across with their shoes tied around their necks.

A Division doesn't move silently across land, nor are they invisible, especially in the daylight.

Minty sees the dust rising in the east, as well as the small deer scampering from the woods are the telltale signs of a large body of men moving through the forest down below. Trouble of the worst kind is brewing.

"Sergeant Fennigan, Minty orders, "pass the word around to eat while they got a chance. Then load and dig in."

The men spend the time after eating waiting, and listening for the picket line to sound the alarm.

A few shots ring out, and the pickets come running up the slope to the Ridge.

Gray clad bodies of men, thousands stretch out, in a long line coming through the woods in the distance

Minty's eyes bulge, at the sight. He yells, "Lt. Davis, have the men pull back across the creek and into the woods, we won't have a chance against that many here. We'll deal with them from there, as they try to cross the creek."

Lt. Davis gallops along behind the line, shouting for the men to pull back. The Rebels, still a long way off, but their nerve wrenching yell can plainly be heard, as they stampede up the slope toward the fleeing Union line.

A few of the men turn to fire futile shots at the charging horde.

Minty orders one of mounted regiments to make a fake saber charge to buy some time.

Captain Henry makes the feint charge, up to top of the ridge, fires two volleys and then rides like hell back towards the creek.

The selfless charge, has bought, Minty's brigade time to escape across the Chickamuaga and gather in the tree line, affording better protection for his men and battery.

Minty, directs his battery officer, to begin firing explosive charges when the Rebels come within two thousand yards. "Don't mistake our cavalry for the Rebs, he warns."

No sooner were those words out of his mouth, when he sees his cavalry come thundering back down the ridge, hell bent for leather.

"Hear they come, won't be long now." Minty says.

The Captain, draws his saber, and orders the battery to load, and stand by.

Colonel Minty hastily rides behind the line, shouting words of encouragement to the men waiting anxiously.

The cavalry unit slows at the approach to the creek and bunches up to cross the bridge.

"Fire!" the battery officer yells.

The artillery pieces belch out fire from the muzzles, sending the iron balls towards their explosive destinations. Pillars of dirt are blasted high in the sky amongst the screaming horde of men bearing down.

Colonel Minty steadies his infantry "Hold your fire until ordered. I want every ball to count."

The battery, however works with deadly speed. Men are torn limb from limb with each encounter from the powerful exploding projectiles.

Jagged pieces of hot shrapnel mow them down in all directions. The tide of men, storming down from the crest of the ridge continues to swell. Smoke from the thousands of muskets shroud the air above the creek, making visibility a problem for Minty directing the fire.

Scores of the Confederates are sent reeling from the deadly fire, and pile up well short of the creek, but their replacements don't miss a step, as they keep driving toward the creek.

The left flank, of Minty's position becomes a concern for the out-numbered, and out gunned brigade. He sends an urgent request for help to Colonel Wilder, who's protecting the Alexander Bridge crossing further to the south.

Colonel Wilder and his mounted brigade are equipped with the new Spencer repeating rifles that have a seven shot rapid fire rate capability. He positions his men to best take advantage of his seven to one advantage. He also has one the best battery commanders in Captain Eli Lilly.

Lilly places his battery hidden underneath large trees but open enough for short range canister shot, as well as long range bombardment.

Eli talking with Wilder, points towards the smoky sky to the north. Wilder gazing at the rising smoke says, "If that smoke starts growing to the northwest we've got trouble."

"Yea and that won't be healthy for my guns."

"Nor will it be healthy for any of us."

Wilder climbs into his saddle and tips his hat, and rides off. He passes by Maj. Lewis, whose walking out of the woods and asks, "Maj. Lewis, post a detail to feed and care for the horses." "Yes Sir. Does the Colonel want me to post a picket line?"

"Here that racket up there to north? We will be seeing the enemy soon enough, Major. Have the men catch some rest while they have the chance."

Sergeant Brammer, cleans the barrel of his Spencer while relaxing with some of the men in his squad, and says "I damn sure would hate to be on the spitting end of this here Spencer, I'll tell ya, boys. Why hell, a well trained squad, could knock off a whole company, with these here rifles."

"Ain't that the truth, as long as ya don't run out of cartridges before they run out of men." Private Newman quips. The remark causes a chorus of laughter among the surrounding soldiers.

"That's very true and real smart, Pvt. Newman. Just so that never happens Private, you've been selected to be our ammunition runner. And trust me Private Newman, no one in this here squad had better ever run out of cartridges."

Wilder, unseen by the Sergeant and the small group of soldiers, laughs under his breath, at the Sergeants response, and whispers to himself, "That Sergeant, is gonna make a hell'va good officer, one day."

He stops his horse and turns around and rides back to the Sergeant and orders "Sergeant, take some men and make a patrol out across the creek, to see if there is any sign of the enemy to our east."

"Ah sir, you want me to lead a patrol, did I hear you right?" Brammer ask.

"You heard right Sergeant."

"Yes Sir! Ok, you bunch you heard the Colonel, now off your asses and get saddled up, right away."

Brammer isn't gone long before he returns at a gallop, and clatters across the bridge up to Col. Wilder.

"Sir, we got Rebs coming thicker than fleas. Best I could tell by all their Regimental flags, it could be at least a Division or maybe a Corp."

"Good work Sergeant. Get your men back in the line, and pass the word to stay down out of sight, and wait for the order to fire. "Major Lewis, get word out to all the regimental commanders to have their men stay undercover out of sight. Be prepared to fight on my signal. If we are outnumbered, surprise will be on our side. Also have Capt. Lilly report to me as soon as he can."

"Yes Sir." Lewis salutes and leaves on the run.

A few minutes later Capt. Lilly reports, and Wilder informs him of the looming threat, suggesting he prepare part of his battery for long distant projectiles and part for canister. He then says, "Captain, if it is a Division we are up against, we won't be able to hold for long. So have your horses harnessed and ready to move on a minutes notice."

A couple of Confederate riders appear, from out of the forest a good distance from the creek. They ride slowly toward the bridge. After a minute or two, they stop some fifty yards short of the bridge, and look around.

Sweat trickles down Wilder's face, stinging his eyes. He wipes the sweat away on his gauntlet, and looks down the line at his men. One can smell the tension building in anticipation. He tries to etch their faces in his memory, for many may be lost this day.

The two riders turn away and gallop back towards the woods.

"My nerves get so damn flustered every time, he remembers. I want to run. Get, before it is too late. John Wilder, you're weak, too damn weak... why can't you get angry, mad, damn it? Please Lord, help me hold myself together and please help me get angry as hell before I jump up and run" he pleads. His tortured agitation is suddenly interrupted when Major Lewis, slides up beside him and hands him his Spencer and a box of cartridges, and says, "I thought you could use this."

Wilder studies him for a second, and replies, "Good thinking Major maybe someday you'll make General."

"I think I'd make a better civilian, Sir."

Col. Wilder examines the woods across the creek through his field glasses. He slowly scans back and forth along the tree line in the distance, looking for the awaited gray scourge to step out from the shadows.

A rider appears, followed by a pair of other riders, with one carrying the Stars and Bars battle flag. A column of riders paired by two's, file out from the trees and into the open. Immediately, a dozen riders, swing out left and right to form a picket line and gallop forward ahead of the rest. The long column continues trailing from out of the forest.

Wilder drops his field glass and quietly says to Major Lewis, "It appears, they haven't discovered us... It looks like only a cavalry regiment, coming to cross our bridge. After we run them off send a detail down to tear up the planking on that bridge. I should have thought of that earlier." Wilder wipes the sweat from his eyes, and puts his field glass away in his leather case. "Put Sgt. Brammer, in charge of the bridge detail."

"Yes Sir. You sort of favor Sgt. Brammer?"

"Yeh, he'll make a good Officer if he lives."

Wilder, feeling fidgety, gets his field glass back out of his case, and focuses on the colonel leading the column. The Colonel's face is smeared with sweat and dust. The men trailing behind are of all ages, some quite young, some a great deal older all lean and dirty.

Wilder feels his hands noticably trembling again. The awful dreaded feeling is returning. He closes his eyes tight. "Dear God not again," he prays to himself. He can see the faces of the men coming to kill him in his minds eye. A change begins to flood over him and down his back. The fear he felt but a second ago suddenly transforms to a feeling of shame. And that makes him mad as hell at his weakness.

Wilder opens his eyes to find his adversary nearing the bridge. Wilder jumps to his feet and shouts "bugler blow your horn!"

The cannons blast several wide swaths of canister shot, ripping through men and horses alike. All down the line, every rifle in Wilder's brigade opens fire on the unfortunate invaders. Men are blasted out of their saddles, and stomped under the hooves of the panicked horses.

The lucky survivors bolted for the safety of the woods.The dust and smoke drifts away, revealing a wretched view of struggling wounded horses with men lying amongst them, torn to bloody shreds. Some are frozen in everlasting peace and others in the throes of painful wounds.

"Major that certainly didn't take long. But I suspect it was only the beginning. You better get the bridge detail moving."

The odor of sulfur hangs heavily in the air, causing ones throat to feel dry and thirsty. I got some water down and figured the horses were in the same boat, so I ordered the men to water their horses.

I damn well knew, for sure, the Rebs would be back. As Sgt. Brammer, put it, "as thick as fleas."

Then it dawned on me, why waste men trying to take a bridge, where they had to bunch up to cross? Hell there is a livestock crossing where the creek shallows not far up the creek. I damn near jump out of my boots and holler for Maj. Lewis. I holler again, but no sign of him. I find the nearest Private and send him to find the Commander of the 98th Ill. because he was at the far north end of our flank.

Down at the bridge, Sgt. Brammer and his squad are busy tearing the planking off the bridge and tossing the boards into the creek where they float away down the creek. Maj. Lewis stands off to the side observing the work, and says "Sergeant we should burn the wood instead of tossing them in the creek." "Maybe, but that could take to long Major.

If those gray back bastards return they could salvage what hasn't burnt. This way they'll have to find them down the creek, God knows where."
"Good point Sergeant, good Point."

Capt. Havensack rides up and reports to Col. Wilder.

"Sir, reporting as ordered."

"Capt., north of your position maybe a half a mile is a ford. Take your Regiment, and do what you can to prevent the Rebs from using it to cross. Do not get yourself trapped, if you face an over whelming situation. Your Spencers is all you got, we don't have time or the resources to supply you with a battery. I repeat, get out if it gets too hot."

CHAPTER 17

Maj. Gen. William Walker confers with Generals Liddell and Walthall, in the woods not far from the Reeds Bridge Road. "Gentlemen, I am catching the blazes, from General Bragg. We need to get possession of the land west of Reeds and Alexander Bridges. Colonel Pegram was repulsed this morning with heavy losses in front of Alexander Bridge. He complained he'd never witnessed such furious rapid fire before. He figures they are using a stacked formation to fire so rapidly. What ever the reason is we need to capture that crossing."

Gen. Liddell breaks in to say "I faced such a fire in Tennessee. They've got new rifles that function like revolvers."

General Walker slowly nods his head, and then continues, "There is an old livestock crossing between those two bridges. I want a Division to get across today. General Hood has taken over the Reeds Bridge operation. He's finding it rough going, and has Johnson and Forrest solving that problem, but said if we could put some pressure south, he feels his opposition will crumble. You two are appointed to solve our problem. So, gentlemen just get us over that damn creek."

Gen. Liddell, salutes and turns his horse away, and rides off with General Whalthall.

"General Liddell, I would be grateful Sir, if you would allow my Division to take a crack at the bridge."

"Edward, that area will need a good barrage from our artillery, covering your attack. You work out the details. I will, take most of the force with me to the cattle crossing. Wait until you hear my guns, before beginning your effort. Take Colonel Pegram's outfit a long with you. He's been there before."

Back across the Chickamuaga Creek, Major Lewis returns with the bridge detail, and reports back to Colonel Wilder informing him the bridge had been dismantled.

"Major, what were you doing with the bridge detail?"

"Ah, Colonel, just making sure the job was done satisfactorily Sir." "Thank you Mr. Lewis, and did Sgt. Brammer, handle the task, to your satisfaction?"

"Yes Sir." "Well good. Now, listen, I posted the 98th Ill. a half a mile north, and I want to move the remaining Regiments up to the creek. You take a Company and move the horses back to the farm behind us. When that's done, join me at the creek.

"Sir, there is no cover at the creek, I just left there."

"Major, If they return, they'll bring artillery, and this time, they will assume we are still hiding in the woods. That's why I want the horses gone. The woods will be a hot spot, until they realize where we are. When that happens, we'll need to move back to the woods fast. I'll need you to direct the covering fire."

"Yes sir Colonel, I'll take care of the horses with B Company, right away."

Colonel Wilder grabs Major Lewis's arm as he begins to leave and says "Send Sgt Brammer, to see me, on your way out."

Sgt. Brammer hustles to see the Colonel, after conferring with the Major. Sergeant Brammer confused by the attention he's been receiving from Col. Wilder, waste no time finding him.

"Sergeant Brammer, I'm promoting you to First Sergeant, congratulations. Your first duty is to inform all Regimental Commanders to move their men to the creek and get down, and stay out of sight. Tell them to commence firing when the enemy gets within the killing range, and not before. You got that?" "Yes Sir". "Good then. Take my horse and I'll see you back at the creek."

Sgt. Brammer, riding the Colonel's horse, passes by his old squad. Corporal Jason who notices, and ask, "you lost your mind, out riding around on the Colonels horse?" "It is now First Sergeant Brammer to you Corporal, now where's the Captain?" Jason points towards a group of men talking underneath a tree, and says "Over there First Sergeant." Brammer remarks "Jason, prepare the squad to be ready to move."

Like a large blue serpent, the two thousand men run out from the trees toward the Chickamuaga Creek. Upon reaching the creek they fall down behind the underbrush lining the creek, obeying the orders to remain down out of sight with no talking.

Wilder glances to the north, and notices the battle smoke there is not as prevalent as before. He pulls out his field glass and searches the woods off in the distance. He's played this waiting game so many times before, and it never gets any easier. The tension builds, and stresses his nerves, but it keeps him tight, alert and ready when the killing begins.

The only sound is the trickling of slow moving water, and the buzzing of insects.

The sound of a cannon report far off across the creek shatters the peace. Then another report after another is heard.

Wilder looks up in time to see the blur of a cannon ball sailing by overhead toward the woods behind him. The blast topples a tree, like a matchstick. His predicted bombardment has begun. He looks back at the trees again to see the explosions erupting all over the woods. Then out of the smoke and dust, he sees Major Lewis and Sgt. Brammer running out of the maelstrom; zigzagging all the way to the creek. Major Lewis's face is white as snow, and his eyes bulging out of their sockets, depicting shear terror. Sgt. Brammer following closely on his heels has the look of a desperate man in search of cover. The pair slides down beside Wilder, gasping for breath.

Wilder lifts up on a knee and says, "You two must be damned indestructible, but time will definitely tell, because here they come."

A shrill scream swells out from thousands of throats, splitting the air over the waiting Union soldiers.

This time, there is a hell of a lot more of them. Five Regimental flags fly at the head the charging horde.

The Union regimental commanders, stationed on the west side of the Creek, steady their men, and wait for the enemy to come into the killing range. The Confederates are already firing as they charge, slowing down to reload.

Colonel Wilder developed a new battle strategy, since procuring his Spencer rifles. Every other man stands and fires his seven rounds, then the second firing line fires while the first reloads. This procedure offers a constant rate of deadly fire.

Capt. Lilly, screams, "Fire!" The artillerymen torch the ports and the cannons jump as the blast sends the balls flying on their way, arching high over the creek and crashing down onto the charging line of Rebels, causing great showers of dirt, steel, and bodies blown up in a nasty cloud of gray and pink vapor. The bombardment continues to pour out the deadly missiles without a let up. The Rebels keep coming, charging through the smoke and horror of it all, moving ever closer to the killing range. Wilder's brigade stays low waiting for the word.

Wilder peers through the underbrush and sees the charging Confederates running toward his concealed line of defense. He struggles against his survival instincts, and resist his impulse to open fire. He vaguely can identify the word, "Mississippi", on one of the fluttering battle flags carried in the hands of a large man running toward him, wearing a gray homespun uniform waist coat. Wilder continues to watch this man coming ever closer. He now can clearly see his face. He knows he must try and kill this man, who ever he is. Somebody's son, or father. The thought is repulsive at first. But then again if it wasn't for this man and people like him, I wouldn't be here, and good men on both sides, would still be at their homes, tending their lives, instead of lying about lifeless. Damn these fool's souls!

Wilder leaps up and screams "fire!"

The once hidden troops rise up, above the foliage, and unleash a storm of lead, felling scores in an instant.

Wilder focuses on the chap carrying the flag and lines him up in his sight. Slowly, he squeezes down on the trigger. The rifle kicks as the large caliber bullet explodes out the barrel. The poor man is knocked backward to the ground, dropping the staff holding the banner. He staggers to recover his balance and the regimental colors. Wilder fires another shot and the unfortunate man doubles over for the last time. His foolish heroic act is his last.

The men stand and fire seven rapid shots at indiscriminate targets, before kneeling down to reload. They are quickly replaced by the second wave of shooters. All the while Capt. Lilly's battery keeps poring on the artillery barrage.

The Rebels, raging charge wavers and slows to a halt.

Col. Wilder, hastily orders the brigade to move back, to the trees, before the Confederates shift their artillery to the creek. The plan he's worked out is working magnificently, as if he could read his enemy's minds. Half his men run for the trees, while the other half covers with rapid fire, before they too hustle back under covering fire. The Confederate artillery damage in the trees has enhanced the defensive positions. Huge craters and felled trees is just what the Doctor ordered.

"Major Lewis", Wilder calls out. Lewis whose uniform is covered with red clay dust, jumps out of a crater, and runs crouching down over to Col. Wilder, whose kneeling behind a felled tree, drinking from his canteen. Wilder lowers his canteen and says "Major, they know where we are now, and I expect they will do something about that real soon. I don't intend on wasting one more man, for a position we eventually won't be able to defend. Send a courier to inform General Thomas, that we will pull back to the LaFayette road, and await his orders."

"What about Col. Minty?" the Major ask.

Col. Wilder points at the smoke high in the sky toward the north, and remarks, "Col. Minty is already pulling back, Major."

The Rebels, have begun charging again through the swirling sulfurous smoke, with their artillery blasting away in the area just beyond the creek.

Col. Wilder sends word down the line for the men to pull back to their horses and form up, ready to move out.

"First Sgt. Brammer, we better move before they discover we're here."
"Yes Col. Wilder, I don't think the two of us can hold here for long."

The Confederates strength is growing across their front, replacing the heavy losses they had sacrificed in front of Col. Wilder's brief but heroic stand.

Their Divisions advance with their flags fluttering in the wind as they file across the creek with every means available.

CHAPTER 18

Maj. General William Walker rides to the foot of the Alexander Bridge on his Dapple Grey horse, to join General Walthall, on the captured bridge.

Walthall sits sadly in his saddle gazing around the ground observing some men caring for the wounded lying helpless among the bloody ones lost forever.

"Gen. Walker, I certainly hope this bridge was worth the price we paid for it."

"General, the price is always too high. Some will write through out history, the Glory of victory has never been free."

"So I suppose, all of this misery, lying here around us, is just a vision of the past and a look at the future."

General Walthall spurs his horse onto the bridge to cross with some of his men. General Walker, calls out, "General wait and hook up with General Hood's Division moving south from the Reeds Bridge." Walthall turns around in his saddle to acknowledge him, from the middle of the bridge, and sadly notices the many tangled remains of those once proud men from Mississippi.

The tenacity from both Col. Minty and Col. Wilder's, small commands have at least muddled Gen. Braggs time table, thus disrupting the coordination of his plan to isolate the Union's XXI Corp.

The creek near Reed's bridge stained red with the blood from the dead slowly meanders south.

Gen. Walker rides over to Gen. Ector, and after a few pleasantries, says "General, we've got to get more men across the creek faster than this. Take your brigade north a mile or two, and cross at Lambert's ford, behind General Liddell's Division. Col. Wilson will follow you across.

General Bragg and his staff ride up. The angry look on his face sours Walker's stomach.

"General Walker, why haven't you got these men across the creek yet?"

"General Bragg, Walker begins the creek is deep, with steep banks. The terrain and roads are rough going as well. Many of my men have worn out shoes. Hell, some haven't any shoes at all. But they still got plenty of spirit and done all we've asked."

"Well General Walker, the sooner you take their spirit over that damn creek and kill some Yankees, the sooner they'll get some damn shoes."

General Walker stares at Bragg with a contemptible look in his eyes. His temper swells within him. He wants to lunge across his saddle and shove Bragg to the ground, and stomp his ugly face into the hard clay ground. But his better judgment takes hold, and he quickly turns his horse and rides off.

General Ector spurs his horse to catch up with him. The two ride together a while saying nothing, until General Walker speaks up, "General Ector, I probably shouldn't say this about our glorious Commander, but I hope, some damn Yankee sharp shooter, blows that ugly old miserable bastard's head off. Ector laughs with Walker, and says, "If his head gets blown off, it probably won't come from a Yankee, I suspect."

"Maybe so, but one can only hope the son of a bitch is buried somewhere, before too long," General Walker curses.

CHAPTER 19

General George Thomas leads his XIV Corp north up the LaFayette Rd, heading to anchor the left flank of Rosecran's three corps. He continues past General Crittenden's XXI Corp that is camped around Lee and Gordon's Mill situated on the Chickamauga Creek, where the creek begins to swing more southwesterly toward the LaFayette Rd.

Col. Wilder visits with General Thomas as he rides along on the LaFayette Rd. in the early evening dark.

Both Wilder and Col. Minty have bivouacked beside the LaFayette Rd, to rest and refit after escaping out of the clutches of Confederate Generals Bushrod Johnson and William Walker's attack on the bridges crossing the Chickamauga Creek.

Wilder reports to Thomas, "General, the Rebels are swarming north of here, and have brought a lot of lead and powder with them. They are definitely angry about that whipping we gave them in Tennessee. I know we were fighting against a Division or more. I couldn't stay long enough to find out exactly. But I know we are facing a good size threat, pretty damn close off to the east of us this evening. Col Minty is presently dug in on my right flank. I fear the Confederates could have, a couple of divisions sitting out there, just too dark to tell."

"Well Colonel, I expected as much, all along. They are far from being demoralized, no doubt. Get yourself rested. I'll try and keep you in reserve for the next day or two if I can. You're one of the best I've got Sir, so rest while you can. Maybe in the mean time we can put a real scare into them."

Colonel Wilder smiles hearing Thomas's compliment and thanks him for his trust. He stiffly salutes the General, and turns his horse around and rides back along the dark road toward his encampment.

General Rosecran moves into his Head Quarter's that occupies a small farmhouse west of the LaFayette Rd on the widow Glen's farm. The farm is not far from, his Corp commanders HQs excepting, General McCook, who is still working his way north.

General McCook, is traveling with his XX Corp over the dark mountain roads, and through the heavily forested trails, well south of General Crittenden's right flank.

Col. Minty, weary and filthy dirty, rides along half a sleep in his saddle, on his way to General Crittenden's headquarters, to debrief him on his experience at the Reed's bridge.

General Crittenden is busy meeting with Gen Thomas Woods, one of his Division Commanders, when Minty arrives. After an informal greeting, Gen. Crittenden takes notice of Minty's uniform, and says, "Colonel, you look the worse for wear."

Minty, embarrassed by his appearance, says, "General, I know, but I fear, the worse is yet to come. General, I'm convinced we are facing a major Confederate push, gathering not far north of here."

Crittenden quietly gets up from his chair, and pours each man a beaker of Brandy, then sits back down.

"How large was the attacking force, you faced at the bridge today" General Woods ask? "Hard to say a Division maybe more, the smoke and dust made it difficult to see clearly" Minty responds.

"Oh come now Colonel, Crittenden interrupts. Hell, I'll bet that rag tag mob couldn't muster enough vagabonds to make a brigade."

Colonel Minty frustrated, by his insinuation, says in a loud voice "General, as I said it was difficult to see most of the time. But their battle flags stand out pretty damn clearly. We faced elements from William Walker's division, and Forrest's cavalry, that I'm sure. A prisoner bragged General Longstreet is on the way.

"That's preposterous, Walker is in Mississippi, and why in God's good name, would they send Longstreet to a theater that is as good as wrapped up, for crying out loud?" remarks General Wood.

"I just know I could make out some of their Regimental flags." Minty responds .

General Crittenden looks intently into Minty's exhausted eyes and says "I can't be sure of what you saw Colonel, but General Wood I need you to ride back with Colonel Minty and find out what's going on."

Colonel Minty slumps in his saddle as he rides along beside General Wood over the dark road, on their way back to his encampment.

Minty and Gen. Wood ride into the camp and are met by the Duty Sergeant. "Good evening Sirs, shall I prepare a tent for the General?" The Sergeant takes the reins of their horses, and General Woods, small but rugged, says "Sergeant that won't be necessary, I've got a bedroll on my saddle and it's a nice night, I'll be fine." "Good Sir, I'll see to breakfast and coffee, when you are ready in the morning."

Colonel Minty, as tired as he is, says "General, I have more than enough room in my tent."

"Thank you, Colonel, but the night air is good for the soul." Col. Minty shrugs, and is not in the mood to argue. "See you then in a couple of hours."

After, Col. Minty walks away, and Woods lays out his bedroll, and takes a minute to peer out at the dark woods across the way in the distance. He lights a cigar, and thinks back at what was said in Crittenden's HQ.

"There's no evidence of camp fires out there. Under his breath he says, "Nah just can't be. There isn't a Reb within miles of here."

General Wood, fast asleep, in his bedroll, is suddenly jolted awake by a loud explosion, followed by others landing all over the place. He jumps out to see muskets flashes a mile long blinking far away in the dark. The General runs to his horse tied to a tree near by. The horse is frantic, dancing and rearing. The Duty Sergeant runs up to Woods and yells, "General I'll get your horse saddled."

Col Minty, with just his trousers and socks on, runs out of his tent, and hollers to the Duty Officer to have "Boots and Saddles blown."

Men race for their weapons, as the skirmish line scrambles back as fast as they can run in the waning dark.

The Sergeant hastily gathers the Generals bedroll, as General Wood straps his saddle on his horse that won't hold still. Woods hollers to the Sergeant "Forget the roll, get to your men, Sergeant. Tell Colonel Minty, I'll get to General Crittenden, and tell him what is up."

"Will do Sir it's best you get though, that lead don't know the difference between stripes or stars."

General Wood, hops around on one foot trying to get his foot in the stirrup, then swings up into the saddle, and spurs his horse in the direction for Crittenden's camp.

Colonel Daniel McCook's brigade is released from General Grangers reserve Corp and ordered to reconnoiter in the vicinity of Jay's Mill, next to Reed's Bridge.

Gen. Bushrod Johnson, by this time has moved his Command south to link up with General Walker. However a small detachment of Georgia cavalry remains in the area.

As would have it, McCook happens upon them along the Reed Rd. Unfortunately for McCook, the younger brother of General Alexander McCook, the XX Corp Commander, is ordered to disengage and return to camp.

The young Colonel, looking for the opportunity, to add a star, takes a circuitous route, to stop and see General George Thomas, to brief and explain how easy it could be to trap the small Confederate force at Jay's Mill.

General Thomas reacts enthusiastically to his report and immediately orders his closest Division, under the Command of General John Brannan to depart for Jay's Mill and capture the wayward Confederates.

Gen. Brannan, roused from his sleep sits on his rumpled cot and reads the communiqué from Thomas. "Alright Major inform the Brigade Commanders to get their men ready to move out, I'll be by to fill them in, as soon as I get dressed."

First Sergeant Hoeppner in the 10th Indiana Regiment, which is part of, Colonel John Croxton's 2nd Brigade, is making the rounds barking out orders "Choke them biscuits down troopers, and get ready to saddle up, we move out in 10." Hoeppner's humor isn't received that well by the men so early in the morning and Deaver speaks up "Damn it Sarge, what's the rush?" Hoeppner who despises back talk snaps, "Corporal you've been told, so move it." Corporal Deavers, to show his disdain, slowly rises and slings what's left of his breakfast across the ground, and cursing "We always get all the shit duty." Private Knaust says, "Deaver, maybe them Rebs are up to something. I thought I heard a commotion earlier off in the distance, and it didn't sound like thunder either."

"Maybe, but that's still no excuse to ruin my breakfast. It ain't right for an army to fight on an empty stomach. Hell, Caesar himself made them rules."

Hoeppner returning from his rounds overhears Deavers and quips, "If you get killed this morning Corporal on an empty stomach you won't bloat, and stink up the damn place."

"That just ain't one of my worries, right now, Sergeant Hoeppner. But Food is!"

Their horses unaccustomed to being disturbed this early are a hand full to control while forming up. Sergeant Hoeppner gets an eyeful from Deaver when he rides by to join the regimental Commander Major Hollis.

Brigade Commander, Colonel Croxton gallops up and joins Major Hollis to tell him to form a skirmish line facing east, while the rest of the brigade will follow some distance behind. He is to proceed with caution and send out a picket line ahead to bait the Confederates. He also informs Hollis, that Col. VanDeveer's Brigade will be covering his left on the Reed's Bridge Rd. "Major Hollis you've got my front, your eyes are our eyes."

Col. Croxton pulls his horse out of the line and turns and gallops back beside the column, and shouts "Glory for the 10th Indiana this day!" They shout back "Hurrah for Indiana!"

Complying with his orders, Major Hollis orders Sergeant Hoeppner to inform Captain Lane to bring his Company forward for Picket duty.

Hoeppner gallops off down the line a short distance and pulls up beside Captain Lane. "Captain Lane Sir, Major Hollis has ordered your Company forward to perform picket duty.

Captain Lane raises his arm and shouts "Company Alpha, follow me to the front… Ho!"

The Company gallops forward past the column and fans out on both the left and right side of Captain Lane.

In front of them a lies a dense forest of shade trees, the ground is mostly free of underbrush.

They ease into the woods, slowly passing through the gaps between the trees. The sun is beginning to rise, but the usual chirping of the birds is mysteriously missing.

Captain Lane carefully guides his horse around a large tree, his eyes scan left and right as they ride ever deeper into the forest.

Private Knaust feeling the tension carefully searches through the trees to his front and notices Corporal Deaver, riding beside him, pull his revolver out, and rest it across the pommel of his saddle.

Knaust nervously fumbles with the flap securing his pistol in his holster.

The only sound heard is the horses shuffling through the carpet of leaves that lies across the ground.

The horses nervous and fidgety tug and jerk at their reins.

Captain Lane raises his arm and quietly signals for the men to stop and dismount. He pulls his revolver out and gingerly moves forward with his horse in tow. One measured step after another, he slowly inches deeper and deeper into the foreboding forest with the picket line.

Ned Deaver, nervous, has stinging sweat trickle down into his eyes, blurring his vision. He glances over at Knaust, whose face appears devoid of color. The muscles in his jaw noticeably twitching.

Suddenly a shot rings out, shattering the tense atmosphere. Captain Lane is flung back against his horse. He momentarily stands there before dropping to his knees, with a stunned look in his eyes, seconds later he topples over face first into the deep bed of leaves.

Appearing out of no where, from a hidden depression, a screaming horde of gray clad horsemen, come galloping out, dodging around the trees blasting away with their revolvers.

Ned Deaver doesn't waste a second, jumping into his saddle, rapidly firing back at the attackers, and hollering as loud as he can, "retreat, retreat!"

Knaust has trouble controlling his panicked horse, and locating his stirrup, before a bullet catches him in his back that spins him around, as another shot slices through his horses neck, spraying a massive vapor of blood over him. Knaust instantly falls to the ground his horse rears and falls on top of him, bathing him in the horse's warm blood.

Ned looks over his shoulder and catches sight of Knaust getting smothered by the flailing horse. He reels around and hurries back and jumps down off his horse, and fires a round at the horses head, killing it instantly. Deavers drops to his knees, holding on to his reins and asks "Knaust can you pull yourself free?" Knaust doesn't move and cries "I can't move Ned!"

Deaver sees the Rebels getting perilously close says, "Lay still then, I'll get back with some help, come hell itself."

Bullets ricochet in the trees close to Deavers. He jumps back on his saddle, and slaps his horse, and races away dodging through the trees, and ducking under the branches.

Major Hollis now keenly aware of the trouble, the pickets have encountered calls for the regiment to split out and form a skirmish line, right and left, then orders them to dismount and prepare for an imminent attack.

The survivors from "Company A" come flying out of the woods, bent low in their saddles, whipping their beast mercilessly, ride to seek the safety of the Regiment. Not far behind them Corporal Deavers gallops for all he's worth to catch up. .

Major Hollis orders Sergeant Hoeppner, "ride out there and fire a couple shot in the air, and let those fools know where the hell we are."

The Sergeant rides forward to a small rise and fires two rounds in the air, catching their attention.

Deavers, pulls hard on his reins, his horse skids to a stop just short of Hoeppner's horse. The Sergeant grabs the bridle of Deaver's horse and hollers, "Corporal, just what in the hell's name, caused this disorderly, and despicable stampede, for Pete's sake?"

Suddenly the Rebels come charging at a gallop out from the woods yelling and screaming like demons.

Major Hollis raises his sword, and screams "Give them hell boys!" The regiment lets loose with a volley of lead that flies into the Rebels with terrible effect. Men are flung out of their saddles and horses cartwheel across the ground from the hail of bullets. The survivors of the first volley turn and race back away for their lives.

Col. Hollis seizes the moment and orders a charge, to hopefully snare the Rebel cavalry before they escape.

Col. Croxton watches through his field glasses from afar, but resists the lure to join in the chase with the rest of the brigade. His experience tells him, that greed can be a fool's share. He'll wait for Col Van Derveer to come abreast on Reed's Bridge Rd.

CHAPTER 20

General Bedford Forrest, sits on his horse; his plumed hat cocked over one eye, wearing an ugly scowl across his face, watches what's left of the Georgia cavalry scramble like rats from a sinking ship. He angrily orders his staff, standing by, "Stop that cowardly rabble and get them formed up to handle a possible counter attack.

General Pegram, the officer in charge of the fleeing Georgia cavalry unit, is the last to return. He sees General Forrest sitting on his horse like a Medieval Prince, reluctant to meet with him, he never the less rides up to report about what happened.

"General Pegram, Forrest begins, if you would sir, go and straighten out that mob you command, and get them turned around, and prepare to face the enemy with some streak of courage. Our illustrious leader, Bragg, would most kindly appreciate it, I'm sure. And General, if that's not possible, I'll a sure you, I'll have all of those yellow bastards charged with cowardice."

General Pegram still somewhat winded from his narrow escape, is furious with the General's tone venomously responds, "General Forrest, this so called mob, bravely pursued a company of Yanks, right into the teeth of a whole damn Yankee brigade. Half of my men are lying back there, to be no more. And what's left will be no more either very soon, if you don't arrange to procure, at least a brigade on this field, to stop what is coming. So arresting them will leave you to fight what's coming all by yourself."

Pegram, glares at him and says no more. He quietly reins his horse around and starts to leave, when General Forrest curtly replies, "General get your men into that hollow, and be ready to take care of business. General Walker is bringing three Divisions here any minute now."

General Pegram nods, and continues to ride away, skeptical of anything Forrest might say.

It's not long though, before Colonel Claudius Wilson arrives with a brigade of five regiments, and moves out into the woods, followed by General Ector, who moves his force further north on to the Reed's Bridge Rd.

General Pegram is able now to breathe a little easier, with the arrival of Walkers reserve Corp.

General Ector marches down Reeds Bridge Road unaware Colonel Van Derveer, and his brigade is marching toward him on the same course sharing the same road.

CHAPTER 21

Col. Chapman another regimental commander in Col. Croston's brigade, ask permission to join Major Hollis.

Croxton's reply was, "No, hold your position we'll wait for Col. Van Derveer to come up along side our left."

"Well sir, Chapman pleads, could I at least set up a defensive line just inside the edge of those trees."

Col. I have no idea, what their strength is at this time, and until I do I … Col. Croxton stops in the middle of his sentence, and thinks for a second then says, Major, if you think it's prudent, you have my permission to go on ahead and proceed into the woods."

Major Hollis, like a bloodhound on the chase, pushes forward into the woods. Corporal Deaver, anxious to get help for his wounded friend Pvt. Knaust rides along with two companions retracing his steps through the woods. Deaver climbs down off his horse and walks through the deep layer of leaves, as he tries to remember where he last saw his friend. They first happen upon the lifeless body of Captain Lane. He pauses there for a minute, to recollect where he was when the first shots were fired. He was over on the left, maybe fifty yards. He hurries off in that direction noisily shuffling through the leaves with his horse in tow. "This way, he's over here", he tells his companions. He spots the rear end of a horse sticking out above the leaves. "Over here, over here." Deaver runs over to the horse's body, where he finds Brandt still alive, but hardly breathing from the weight of the dead horse on him. Deavers leans over and says, "Brandt your worries are over now, I've got help with me to get this damn horse off ya. I'll have you out of here before you know it."

Brandt manages a little smile, and whispers, "Ned I knew you'd be back."

"Don't you worry none boy, you'll be free in a minute."

The other two are standing by silently waiting. Deaver stands up and tells them to get his horse and attach the line to his saddle, and the other end around the dead horse's hind legs. "Get my horse started and I'll pull Brandt at the same time." They prepare the rope, and Deaver grabs a hold of Brandt's arms and hollers "now!" The soldier slaps Deaver's horse, and the dead horse's body slides off Knaust and Deavers quickly pulls on Brandt's arms. Brandt lets out a horrid scream, and then just as quickly becomes lifeless. Ned whispers, "hey we gotcha free, you'll be just fine now." He leans over to comfort him, when he notices the color has left his face, and his eyes are fixed half open, with the look of death.

Corporal Deaver studies Brandt's ashen face. He gingerly lifts Brandt's head and places his cap on, buttons his collar and folds his arms over his chest. Satisfied that Private Knaust looks his best, Ned stands and picks up Brandt's carbine, and says to his two companions, "we best catch up with the regiment."

Deaver and his two companions soon arrive back into the fold, with Major Hollis, and the Company, moving peaceably through the wilderness, confident they have the upper hand.

Colonel Wilson moves with his Georgia boys into the same woods as his enemy. His five regiments stretch out for some six hundred yards. The three regiments on his right, soon to come into contact with Major Hollis's regiment slowly probing through the woods.

Mini balls from both sides fill the air, slamming into man and beast alike.

Screams, mixed with the angry sounds of men locked in close combat, claw at the pit of every man's stomach.

Major Hollis's regiment out gunned and overwhelmed calls for an orderly retreat. The Indianans begin firing and falling back, until they run short of cartridges. Men start dropping by the score on both sides, either killed, or badly wounded. Deaver scours through dead men's cartridge boxes for ammunition. He loads his revolver on the run then spins around in the knick of time, to fire two rounds into the chest of a Reb, before the Reb tries to run him through with his bayonet. Deaver, keeps firing at the wave of men running him down. Disparate for ammunition, he searches the dead, loads, fires and searches again. All the while, he miraculously escapes harm or capture. Exhausted by the strain of battle, and separated from his company, he becomes complacent to his plight. Nothing really matters now. Death would be a relief. Dropping to his knees, he attaches a bayonet to a rifle he finds, and jams the butt into the soil and braces, for the next act. Ned closes his eyes, as the sounds of battle around him become muffled. His mind slows, and his anxiety dissolves, leaving him in a dream like state. No longer concerned whether he lives or dies, his fate will be what it may. White wisps of smoke swirls about his exhausted body, as he lies motionless with his back to the ground.

Colonel Croxton loses his composure and screams for his men to wheel about to the right when his flank becomes threatened, as his brigade teeters on the brink of disaster under the weight of the Georgia boys.

Colonel Hays and his 10th Kentucky react quickly to wheel around to the south. His swift response is in time too slow Wilson's brigade down a bit.

General Brannan, some distance away watches the battle, through his binoculars. He scans to the left, where Colonel Van Derveer on the Reed's Bridge Road, is hotly engaged against a swarming body of determined Texas cavalry.

Smoke lies heavily over the area, making it very difficult to make command decisions.

Brannan, never the less, decides to send in his reserves, half of them to Van Derveer, and the other half to Croxton. He then sends an urgent request to General Thomas for help.

CHAPTER 22

General George Thomas stands at his map table in his headquarters when the courier from General Brannan, arrives, and hands the General the message. The message reads, "Heavily engaged, reserves committed, outcome doubtful, if not supported quickly."

Thomas has been aware of the trouble to the east, since it began this morning, and has already studied the disposition of his Corp. Thomas orders General Absalom Baird's 1st Division, to move at once, and coordinate with General Brannan.

General Baird waste little time, to meet with Brannan. Brannan informs him, the reserves he rushed to Croxton and Van Derveer, has slowed the Confederates advances some. If Baird could push a brigade to the right of Croxton's position, and another over to the right of Van Derveer, the contest should be settled favorably.

Baird, orders Col. Scribner, with his First brigade to attack the Rebels left flank off Croxton's right. He sends his other brigade, General King's Third brigade to support Van Derveer's right.

Colonel Scribner with slashing speed slams into Wilson's left flank, cutting the heart out of the assailants. The failure of Wilson's left, contaminates, his whole line.

General King proceeds north a mile through the dense woods and punches into Ector's left side.

King's batteries at first opened up and weaken the Texans with a terrible storm of bursting shells spraying iron and wood splinters everywhere.

Ector knows he is facing certain death if he remains there much longer. The jagged missiles pour down on them like rain. Some try to flee and run into the muzzles of King's advancing infantry. The Federals, rout of the Confederates, takes only a very short time that leaves a vast area of torn corpses. An eerie quiet, settles over the dead.

Long lines of haggard gray clad troops shuffle westward under the watchful eyes of their Yankee guards.

Fortunate or unfortunate, their nightmare is over.

Croxton's brigade, on the move since before daylight is in need of rest, replenishment, and ammunition. General Brannan thus orders them back across the LaFayette Rd to get refitted

CHAPTER 23

Corporal Deaver, struggles to make his way through the woods, his face blackened by gunpowder, looks as ragged as he feels. A couple of soldiers from the 38th Indiana find Deaver with his head bleeding, lying among several dead Confederates. The two soldiers help him to his feet, and steady him. The three men need to step over the mangled body of a Southern soldier, crumpled across a fallen tree. Deaver staggers some when he reaches down to grab a canteen off the dead soldier's body. He pulls the plug out of the neck and slurps the water like a desperate animal, spilling as much water as he drinks down. Stopping to take a breath, he notices the expressions on the other two men staring at him. He then returns the canteen to his mouth and gulps some more, after which he throws some over his face. Deaver tosses the empty canteen back on the body of the dead Reb, and says, "Water is still water, no matter whose it is. I haven't eaten a crumb either, since God knows when. But them Rebs aint got nothing worth eating, the poor bastards."

One of the soldiers with Deaver is a Sergeant, a little older than Ned. The other, a Private, who appears to be much younger.

The Sergeant puts his hand on Ned's shoulder and says, "Corporal, come on, we'll get you back, where you can rest and be fed. Then I'll help you find your own outfit." Ned nods, and says, "That will be mighty kind of you Sergeant. We gotta get the hell out of here now anyhow, before these ole boys begin to swell and smell up these here woods around here." A queer look is born across Deaver's face suddenly, thinking, somewhere back there, Brandt lies breathless in this lousy wilderness, deep in the leaves, just like the rest of these poor lost sons of mothers lying here.

Corporal Deaver, and his new companions sit, with their backs against a caisson wheel enjoying a generous portion of bacon and biscuits. Unlike his Sergeant in the 10th, this Sergeant, understands the needs of his men. He's given Deaver a new cap, canteen, and a sack full of cartridges.

Deaver sets his empty tin on the ground, and says "a fellow could sure get use to this fine living. I could sure use a Sergeant like you in the 10th. The young soldier sitting next to him remarks, "The Sergeant and me grew up together, his name is Jim, and he's my brother." Deaver looks at both of them, the youngster his blond hair down across his forehead, doesn't look a thing like his brother. The younger brother continues to say "back home Jim is everybody's friend including many orphaned animals, he has adopted." "Yea, he's a hell of a nice man alright." Deaver said as he closes his eyes to rest.

CHAPTER 24

General St. John Liddell's Division with four thousand men step out in a long single line of battle, cutting northwest across the Brotherton Rd, with General Walthall on the right and Colonel Govan on the left. His mix of troops from Arkansas and Mississippi silently make their way through the woods, staying low to sneak across a large open field just east of the woods where two Ohio regiments lounge about on the western edge of the open field.

Colonel Scribner's men are feeling rather good after overwhelming Wilson's Confederates the way they did, and haven't as yet posted their pickets.

The hot breath of Braxton Bragg is beginning to make Rosecran sweat a bit. Convinced that his left is the main target of Bragg's wrath, he sends General Thomas two Divisions from McCook and Crittenden's Corp, to bolster his left.

Rosecran's dice has been coming up with lucky Sevens all summer, But he is having a hard time accepting the idea that Bragg is getting stronger with new replacements, thus the proverbial Seven could be harder to come by.

General Baird rides over to confer with General Brannan at his headquarters. The two pour over their map and chart their forces exact positions around the area. General Baird points to a gap between Scribner and General King's brigade, and says, "I don't like the distance between these brigades because we've lost our continuity there." Brannan remarks, "Uh, I see something else that is bothersome. So far, they've come at us from the northeast of our lines, forcing us to strengthen our positions there. If I were Bragg, I would change that and hit our line in the center, and then push northwest to try and divide us. I hope General Thomas is considering that possibility." General Baird shakes his head and says, "I'll get word to him to that effect, and pull Scribner's brigade back in line with King, at least until we hear something from General Thomas."

Deaver is abruptly shaken from a deep sleep, by a loud explosion, not far from where he is lying. Instinctively he grabs his carbine and sits up, squinting through his blood shot eyes, to see soldiers running about the camp in complete pandemonium. Sergeant Jim stands near by, barking orders to the panicked men to grab their rifles and fall in. Deaver jumps up and runs through the dust of a near explosion, over to Jim, who is covered in dust from the same blast. "Hey, Sergeant, where in the hell is the enemy?" Jim hollers above the din, "Corporal, you need to get the hell back to your unit, over to west of here. The Rebs have broken through our lines east of here." Deaver stares into his new friend's eyes and says, "Sergeant the fight is here and here is where I'll fight." Jim grabs Deaver's shoulder and with a big grin, says, "Corporal, I like the cut of your jib, we'll do this together then."

Once again Deaver is thrust into the middle of the lions den, with a Lion's share of trouble.

General Walthall, commanding Liddell's Confederate right wing is the first to make contact with Scribner's leading regiments. His Mississippi boys pounce with frightful fury against the two unsuspecting Ohio regiments, and instantly destroy nearly half their number, sending the rest scurrying for the rear.

Liddell, leading his left wing, against General Starkweather's brigade, catches them napping as well. An awful bloodletting spills through the ranks of the Union brigade. The thrust is so quick, the boys in blue, are unable to mount any kind of a defense against the fast charging Rebel force from Arkansas.

Ned Deaver fighting along side Sergeant Jim and his brother, is knocked dizzy, from the butt end of a rifle swung to his head, and then is stabbed with a bayonet to his hip as he falls. His mind swirls in a fog, he vaguely, catches sight of the bloodied Sergeant Jim falling on the body of his young brother.

Advancing unmolested, the Graybacks reach the rear of General King,s brigade before he can turn his guns around.

King now gets a taste of what he dished out to the Confederates earlier.

King's men are forced back into the safety of General Van Verdeer's alerted brigade. Van Verdeer's defenders ignore the panicked soldiers running through their ranks, and sternly dig in and wait for the frenzied disorganized horde of Rebels closing in from the south.

General Brannan raises the ante and orders the proud all German regiment under Colonel Kammerling into the fray against the Mississippians.

Straining to get into the fight, Kammerling plunges head long into ranks of the exhausted Mississippians, and stops them in their tracks.

Inspired by Kammerling's audacity, other regiments jump out of their defense and join in the melee.

General Walthall loses the cohesion between his units on the right and becomes painfully vulnerable by this reversal. Battered and bleeding they begin to lose all the ground they had gained. General Liddell's collapsing right puts his left in jeopardy of getting ground to a pulp as well.

General Brannan calls on the refitted Croxton to get back into the fight and challenge Liddell's struggling left.

Croxton double times into the exposed Rebel flank. His 10th Kentuckians wade in slashing and stabbing the hapless boys from Arkansas in a murderous frenzy.

Liddell has no choice, but to order a general retreat to avoid further slaughter.

General Walker slumps in his saddle, as he listens to the sound of the battle become louder as it changes directions. The telltale sign his soldiers are in a retreat.

General Walker says, to General Forrest watching from his horse beside him, "What a waste, we should have pulled back into the mountains where we could at least be more effective." Forrest responds rather dryly, "General I ain't much for defending ground, I'm all about taking it." General Walker sighs and replies "I agree with you General, if you have the resources and that is something we do not have." "Maybe, Forrest continues, but you let me move my old command, to the north under cover, and hit them Yanks where they aren't looking, instead of where they are.

"You see Colonel Dribrell could use the low ground north of Reed's Bridge Rd. That will enable him to stay under cover until he reaches a position off their flank, from there he can strike with snake like speed. My boys can be real damn ruthless, that I can promise you."

General Walker sits silently, staring off in the distance, while he ponders Forrest's suggestion.

"General Forrest, I'll lay down an artillery barrage to the south to distract them, at the appropriate time."

CHAPTER 25

Sergeant Hoeppner returns with his men from a search for wounded among the bodies of both sides, strewn over the ground when he comes upon Ned Deaver, bleeding from his wounds lying amongst them. "Well, well, well, now if this ain't something, my old Corporal Ned Deaver. Thought you'd done got yours this morning." Hoeppner said. Deaver struggles to speak, "I'm afraid not, Sergeant, and I see, you've managed to stay well all the while." "For sure Corporal and I see you're still lying down on the job as usual" Hoeppner says sarcastically. "Just sitting around, waiting to see your ugly face again." Deaver replies. "Well Corporal lets see if we can't find you a more comfortable place, to look upon my face."

"Where you hit Corporal?" Deaver closes his eyes and says, "Don't know for sure. Think I got stabbed in my right hip, and bashed in the head." "You shot anywhere boy?"

"I don't think so." "Then get the hell up and lets get going." "Wish I could, but I can't move my leg."

Hoeppner, sees the blood soaked trouser and hollers out to a couple of privates near by, "you men stretcher this man back to the aid station, and don't dilly dally about it either. Deaver, you'll be back safe and sound in Chattanooga, lying about, doing what you do best" Hoeppner growls.

Deaver lays back and sadly glances over at the bodies of his two friends, Sgt. Jim, with his arm lying over his younger brother.

Both General Baird and Brannan have learned a lesson or two this morning. Victory has lately been ever fleeting, and they need to hastily reform and prepare for a counter attack. They are deep in the south and the enemy is desperate and committed.

Colonel Dribell leads a couple thousand of tough Tennessee soldiers, down a wooded ravine as quiet as mice. Slowly Dribell crawls up the slope to check his position. He peers through his binoculars, and sees a city of white tents in the distance. Dribell signals for his men to climb the slope and stay low.

Colonel Van Derveer has taken the precaution to prepare a defense in case of a surprise attack from the north. He has two batteries of three cannon each ready for that event.

Colonel Dribell orders the charge. The men rise up and charge over the top, screaming their blood curling fiendish yell.

The yanks run to their batteries and quickly charge the guns with powder and six pound explosive balls. The infantry also races to meet the threat. Cannons blast their deadly missiles into the raging mass of charging men. Huge geysers are blasted into the air, creating a ghastly portrait of reds and gray plumes floating in the swirling wind. Men just disappear into a pink mist.

The ranks of the charging Confederates are swooped away leaving alleys of empty space once occupied by men only seconds before. Rank after rank is relentlessly blown away in the maelstrom.

The table turned against him, Dribell calls for his men to retreat back to the safety of the wooded ravine.

General Thomas rides up to join Van Derveer to congratulate him for running the Rebels off. Thomas raises his field glass and catches sight of one of the last Rebels, struggling to hobble from the nasty field.

"Colonel, I'm sending you some ammunition wagons to replenish your needs." "Thank you General, I could use more… General can I speak freely Sir?" "Yes of course, what's on your mind, Colonel?"

"General, I got lucky today, damn lucky. I had a premonition, you might say, to prepare, in the event we might get attacked from the north." "Well Colonel, you call it what you may, but that's why you have those Eagles sewn on your shoulder."

Van Derveer blushes, and more abruptly states, "General, I don't think we are doing this right. I mean Sir, we are getting attacked here and there, and we have successfully repulsed them so far. But that's just it. We should be attacking with one cohesive force, all at once, with all three of the Corps involved at same time. Instead, we continue to make the same mistake they are making."

General Thomas stares at him for a minute while he considers what he just heard and, says, "interesting point of view Colonel."

Thomas slips his glass back into it's case and sticks a cigar between his teeth, turns his horse away and says before departing, "Colonel, you Sir, are our cornerstone here on the left. It's of the utmost importance for you to stay vigilant I fear our enemy is getting reinforced by the train load."

CHAPTER 26

General Bragg curses as he looks at the map to see what success his forces have accomplished. He's extremely aggravated, with the news arriving from the field. An unlucky staff officer standing by taking notes at the map table catches his ire.

Bragg raises up from the table, with an expression of displeasure on his face, sniffs, and bitterly exclaims to the officer, "You stink! You crap your britches, boy?"

The startled officer steps back, blushing. "Get the hell out of here and clean yourself up. How can I concentrate with the stench of you? Get the hell out of this house!

You are no longer on this staff, you hear?" Bragg yells.

The embarrassed officer sheepishly backs away and hurries out of the headquarters and shuts the door. Bragg still not giving up on the subject continues his rampage, "Major Channing, send that fool to a fighting unit, I don't want him around smelling up my headquarters, you hear." Yes sir General. Channing replies.

"Also Major, get me a report on the progress of General Cheatham's Division, he should be in position by now. Also get me some news on General Longstreet's where abouts." "Yes Sir, right away General." The Major, takes a step toward the door, when he too, experiences Braggs vile nature "Major, not you damn it, I need you here. Send couriers Major, he yells, and then mumbles, I'm surrounded by idiots, and God knows what else."

CHAPTER 27

General Cheatham's Division arrives none too soon to rescue General Walkers bleeding force.

It's now early afternoon and the situation is critical. General Walker's Corp has failed in every attempt to come out on top.

As has been the case thus far, Cheatham isn't given the time to organize a plan of action. Once again, to put it metaphorically, Cheatham will have to put the cart before the horse.

Hot spots of combat are still smoldering here and there through out the woods. Colonel Croxton's brigade in Brannan's Division was in the forefront, and Walkers Confederates, though falling back and slow to do so, they have plenty of venom left to strike again.

General Cheatham leads off with General John Jackson's five regiments. Jackson aware that friendly forces are still actively engaged to his front moves cautiously up the Alexander Bridge Road, careful to avoid mistaking friend for foe.

A courier rides up to inform Jackson, that yanks are positioned in a tree line, not far from his front. Jackson immediately orders his regiments to fall out right and left to form a single line of battle, and continue toward the woods ready to meet the Yanks.

Colonel Chapman, commanding the 10th Indiana, orders Sergeant Hoeppner to pass the word down the line, to hold their fire until instructed.

Watching the marching line of Confederates close the distance is painfully nerve racking.

Sergeant Hoeppner sets his sight on a rather large Sergeant wearing a yellow chevron on his dirty gray sleeve. Step after step the stranger in the slouch hat, becomes a little larger with each step. Hoeppner's no rookie to war and still feels the excitement of the hunt. He slowly cocks the hammer on his musket, and steadies his sight. Sweat drips off his nose.

Chapman passes another order down the line, "fire one volley and pull back to establish a defense line in the woods. He refocuses on his target after passing along the order. He knows patience belongs to the hunter, and surprise belongs to the hunted.

The musket jumps, fire and smoke belch out the barrel, the Sergeant with the yellow chevron, head explodes in a shower of blood. Shouts of "fall back, fall back, radiates through the air, as the men in blue run with all they got to get to the woods and set up their defense.

Laboring to catch his breath, Hoeppner flops to the ground and struggles to get his ramrod free. Seconds later he rams a ball down the barrel atop a wad of powder. He shouts, "Fix bayonets and Reload!" Soldiers their fingers trembling fumble with their ramrods as they hurry to reload.

Colonel Croxton has his hands full, when General Cheatham feeds more and more troops into the fight.

Hoeppner, reloads and fires like clockwork at the screaming rebels. Desperation pushes fear aside and reality sets in. Suddenly, above the din of battle, he hears the sound of running footsteps too his rear. He twirls around and levels his bayonet.

To his surprise, thousands of blue uniformed men are weaving their way through the trees, running right toward him.

Johnson's Division, along with Palmer's is charging in to meet the enemy.

Cheatham's center gets forced back, across a cleared field leaving their dead and wounded sprawled across the ground. They pull back to regroup. Exhausted, and low on ammunition confederates drop down on the sandy soil to wait for the killing to begin once again.

Two brigades from General Van Cleve's Division, from General Crittenden's XXI Corp, hustle at double time north along the LaFayette road. Winded by the sprint they enter the woods on the right of General Palmer's position who is by now heavily engaged fighting off a rebel attempt to turn his right flank. That Rebel threat comes from General Wright, who was sent by Bragg to bolster General Cheatham.

Both sides feed the "Beast", like piling wood on top of wood in a fire pit. Men are thrust into the jaws of death, piling bodies on bodies.

The smoke is so thick over the ground commanders to lose sight of where they are. The black powder smoke mixed with woods set afire from explosive sparks, obscures visibility to a point of feet, not yards.

Generals Bragg and Rosecran play a deadly game with men's lives. Bragg raises the pot and antes Alexander Stewarts Division. Rosecran counters with General Joseph Reynolds Division. Bragg grows the pot with Hood's Division, featuring Busrod Johnson, and Evanders Laws Brigades. Rosecran calls, with General Jefferson C. Davis Division, no kin to the Southern President.

The game is on, and the Southern heavy weight, General Longstreet, the famed star of many Virginia exploits with Robert E. Lee, is on his way to sweeten the pot once again.

CHAPTER 28

By three o'clock in the afternoon, a fissure opens in the Union center, where two Tennessee brigades, break through and cross over the LaFayette road, pushing the Federal commander, Colonel Edward King back, creating a gap of some 600 yards, between Reynold's and Davis's Divisions.

General John Hood's entry into the fray is overwhelming the under strength Union center.

Corp commander, Crittenden, directs General Thomas Wood to take two brigades north via the LaFayette road, and report to General Van Cleve.

Navigating the road is easy, but locating Van Cleve, in the dense smoke and a half a day of troop realignments from battle situations, General Thomas Wood has an impossible task to find anything except trouble.

General Wood, riding at the head of his column, comes upon a formation of Union soldiers waiting on the road for instructions from General Davis. Beside the road is a piece of farmland that features a rather large clearing in the midst of the wilderness, called Viniard field.

Several Confederate regiments from Hood's Corp are regrouping in the woods beyond the field to the east. General Davis, has already dealt with the threat earlier, and is discussing plans with General Carlan for a renewed attack, when he notices General Wood, riding towards him.

General Wood swings down from his horse and greets Davis with a smile and friendly handshake, instead of the customary salute.

"What's going on General?" Wood inquires.

"I damn sure got my hands full General. Those woods across the way are crawling with Rebs. All I've got is two brigades. I'll tell ya, we've got hell to pay here.

General Wood, sensing Davis's anxiety, considers his orders from Crittenden; should he continue on to locate Van Cleve, or stop here and throw in with Davis?

He decides the right thing to do in this case, is to back Davis.

A courier hastens up to Davis with an urgent plea from one of his brigades commanders Colonel Heg, asking for reinforcements to be sent up the road to his left, or else the enemy might gain his rear.

General Wood is quick to grasps the situation and orders his leading brigade Commander Colonel Harker to attack the enemy crossing the LaFayette road to the north. Harker, first, needs to push through Carlan's disorganized troops scattered over the road, after retreating from the Viniard field.

Harker hasn't far to go before he makes contact with the men in gray.

All hell breaks loose, as the Blue and Gray mix it up in close, man on man combat. Soldiers from both sides wade in firing, slashing, clubbing, and stabbing, using anything and everything that's available at hand. The blood runs hot, and the desire to survive trumps, the fear of death.

Colonel Harker's fresh Brigade and the infusion of Colonel Wilder's troopers joining in with their Repeaters are too much for the battle weary boys in Gray. The dead, the dying and the wounded lay in heaps, co-mingled with their enemies, joined together in blood.

For now the stability along the Union line on the LaFaytte road is reestablished in the Union's center.

Half mile south in the Viniard field, the situation for the Union is of a different color, all mixed up.

Colonel Barnes leading the other brigade of General Wood's division is ordered into the field off Carlan's right. He mistakenly marches his four regiments out in front of Carlan's field of fire. Carlan's regrouped brigade is involved in a heated bout with a Confederate brigade trying to take over the field.

Barnes, his colorful regimental banners fluttering in the breeze, proudly marches out on the field to do battle for the first time today. However, he is marching in the wrong direction.

Colonel Carlan goes berserk and is beside himself in disbelief, as he watches Barnes commit this intrusive maneuver. Carlan screams out, "What the hell is he doing? For God's sake, can't he read his damn compass?"

Barnes is headed northeast instead of east, and cuts right in between two opposing brigades.

The Southern commander at first is confounded, to see the Union brigade's flank parading across his front. Never has he had prey jump right in his lap like this before.

Patiently, he sits and waits, hiding behind high brush along a fence, separating the field from the woods. He waits for his enemy to come perpendicular with his line of fire.

Finally, he hollers, "Fire!" The Confederates open up, pouring out a murderous enfilading sheet of fire, into the defenseless Yanks.

The unsuspecting Federals are massacred like cattle in a slaughterhouse.

The terrible suddenness from the Rebel fire causes a panic to flood through the four regiments, sending the survivors stampeding through Carlan's brigade, and thus creating a terrible panic to run amuck in his ranks, that sends his men into flight as well.

Carlan, infuriated, at the sight of his men, running away, screams curses at them, for their cowardly behavior. But the fever reaches a high pitch, and his once proud brigade, dissolves in front of his eyes.

Colonel Twigg, the Southern Commander, on the fence, that has just caused the death of many healthy young lads, in Blue, spontaneously reacts to the federals retreat and orders his four regiments "over the fence to get the hell after them yellow bastards."

His Commander, General Hood, not informed and unaware of Trigg's impulsive order, has sent word for Trigg's Brigade to turn right and slide to the north. This lack of communication with Trigg, has a devastating effect on his far left regiment, which doesn't receive the word.

This ill-informed regiment, immediately jumps over the fence and enters the field confident they will be joined with the others, proudly march in line of battle, unaware they alone are racing to defeat a Yankee Division.

In the meantime, the LaFayette road is a scene of complete pandemonium. The road, congested with soldiers milling about disorganized, are ripe for the picking.

General Wood, disgusted by this collapse in discipline, personally storms in amongst the crowd, shouting curses, and shoving men around, trying to get some order. He grabs a Lt. Colonel, and screams in his face, "Get some order here, or shoot any son of a bitch, who refuses to listen, do you hear."

Colonel Buell however has managed to maintain discipline and order among his troops, in this caustic situation.

General Wood, orders Buell not to waste a minute and get back into the field, and avenge the disgraceful rout of Colonel Barnes's soldiers.

Colonel Wilder not under General Wood's authority decides on his own initiative to join Colonel Buell, with two of his regiments.

The lone Confederate regiment that ventured onto the Viniard field is overwhelmed, and easily swept away, by the avenging six Union regiments.

Wilder, his blood running hot, halts in the middle of the chase, when he notices the volume of smoke increasing over Barkers way.

Wilder expertly turns his men north and rides to where the action is.

The Supreme Court Justice from Georgia, Colonel Benning, and his Georgians have taken the stage along side General Robertson, for another effort at splitting the Union line on the south sector.

The Southerners however, quickly run head long, into a curtain of steel, gratis Colonel Wilder's Repeaters.

The odds against seven shots to one shot, paints a grim picture for the underdog, and no sane man wants to be left out in the open under those circumstances.

A dry five foot deep ditch offers the only sanctuary near by, from the deadly fusillade. The desperate Confederates scurry into the ditch, painfully piling on top of one another. Poor Private Darby screams as a large man jumps on his face, smashing his nose. His blood gushes out as if he was shot in the face. Scores of others get injured by their fellow comrades, who frantically seek safety in the deep ditch. The crowding makes it nearly impossible to perform the necessary steps to reload their muskets. Sticking one's head above the ditch to fire on the Yanks is dangerously necessary to defend the position against assault.

Colonel Wilder concocts a solution to negate the protection the ditch provides for the isolated Confederates.

Under fire, Wilder directs Eli's battery around to face directly down the ditch along with one of his Spencer equipped regiment.

A young Confederate Officer notices the enemy soldiers setting up, paralyzed by the sight and he can't get the words out of his mouth to warn of the impending slaughter. He desperately grabs the shoulder of the man next to him and swings him around, pointing at the Union formation. The very next second, a Union Six Pound cannon ball is speeding towards them. The ball misses the young Officer, but instantly takes the head off the soldier he was trying to alert. The ball continued its deadly flight, striking a half dozen men further down, killing them all, before they knew what hit them.

The young Officer, instinctively claws his way up the steep bank to escape the death trap. Once over the top he attempts to run, and is shot two or three times, before his body flops to the ground.

The ferocious fire of leaden missiles, sweeps down the ditch, killing all in its path. To remain in the ditch means certain annihilation. The lucky ones scrambled out of the ditch, to take their chances running unprotected out in the open, in search for some other shelter.

The disorganized remnants left from Benning's and Robertson's brigades escape as best they can for the safety of the woods, whence they had come.

The little Irishman, General Phil Sheridan arrives with his 3rd Division, from McCook's Corp, with orders to reinforce General Davis. General Sheridan seizes the opportunity to immediately act and get after the retreating Rebels, racing east through the Viniard field.

Like a cornered wounded animal, the Rebels have no intention of giving up, and have every intention to make the Yanks pay dearly for every one of the Sons of the South they have sent to the great beyond.

Sheridan, doesn't get far before he feels their bite, and quickly reverses his decision, recalling his Division before they suffer emore harm.

Colonel Wilder's stalwart Brigade noticed by the other units, for their courage and discipline under fire, inspires many of the disheartened soldiers, that renews their courage. These same defeated men, who had run away out of shear terror, now begin to filter back to find their units. Restored of their self worth, they step back in side by side with the survivors.

One such soldier unashamedly remarks, "When the fellers started falling all around me, I knew it was best I be getten, if I wanted to be around another day." The other soldier listening agrees. "I know what you mean. I saw Colonel Heg get his, and then I saw the others begin to high tail it, so hell, I done lit out myself. I didn't exactly cotton to getting kilt.

CHAPTER 29

Dusk is slowly setting across the eastern sky, while both opposing Armies begin posting their pickets, along the boundaries on opposite sides of Viniard field.

White flags, carried by the burial parties, collect their dead strewn across the field. Horse drawn freight wagons silhouetted against the pink horizon, stand idly by, and wait to be loaded with the grizzly harvest.

Campfires spring up like fireflies throughout the darkening woods.

An eerie peace settles over the Viniard field.

Not far to the north, a mile or so, the scene is much the same.

General Thomas, takes advantage of the respite to visit with his subordinate Commanders and inspect his lines.

Thomas rides along with his old trusted sidekick, Sergeant O'Sullivan, in search of General Richard Johnson's Division. He feels uneasy, as they ride further and further in the dim wilderness, far from his main line. After what seems like an hour, they encounter a courier on a message run from Johnson's camp. The Courier points the direction to Johnson's encampment, before riding off.

General Thomas's first order of business upon arriving at Johnson's Headquarters is to order him to move his Division west back towards the main line, and dig in beside Palmers left flank.

In a hurry to get to Rosecran's Headquarters, before dark, Thomas is off again riding through the darkening woods, towards the Widow Glen's house, a couple of miles to the southwest.

On his way, he happens upon General Brannan, who is out checking on his brigades.

"General Brannan, good evening Sir, I was hoping to catch up with you, before I meet with General Rosecran.

General your lines are spaced nicely, except, I need you to move Colonels King's brigade closer toward General Negley on your right. We've got a quarter mile gap there between the two of you, and that has to be closed up."

"General Thomas, my men have built defensive works along their front, after one tough day of fighting. They are worn a bit thin, I'd sure hate to ask them to move again." "General Brannan, the whole damn Corp has been shot to pieces today. And you can bet, they are just as tired. You convince your men, their best chance to see another sundown, will be to do as they ordered, and do it tonight.

One other thing General, have your Commissary cook up two days ration of bacon for each man, along with plenty of sugar and coffee; want to keep them sharp in this heat. We'll need to get all we can from them."

"General Thomas, Brannan says, pausing to collect his thoughts, before continuing, "You know we came within a whisker of loosing the line today. But we charged back and slammed the door in the bastards face. They're going to be fed all the bacon and, biscuits they can stomach by God."

Thomas, laughs, tips his hat, and rides away.

CHAPTER 30

General Thomas has been pushing himself hard all day, from dark to dark. He's tired, disheveled, and dirty. He hasn't washed in a couple of days, and smells of smoke, horse, and sweat. He slides down out of his saddle, and hands the reins to an orderly. Sergeant O'Sullivan does the same. They brush the dust from themselves, and walk over to step up on the porch. O'Sullivan stops, and says, "General, I'll leave you here to your business Sir, if the General won't mind. I won't be but a shout away, if you're in need of me. "Sergeant O'Sullivan, your service will not be needed for awhile, you go ahead, and get what you need out of your saddlebag."

"Well, that tis mighty kind of you General Sir, and hope you take a wee bit inside for yourself."

General Thomas steps through the door, the room is busy, and crowded with Staff Officers.

General James A. Garfield catches sight of Thomas from across the room, and hurries over to greet him.

Rosecran, busy studying a map tacked on the wall, looks over his shoulder, and hollers, "General, just the man I need to verify some information on our troop disposition in your sector. But first, let me just say, I was definitely wrong, I should have listened and heeded your warning in Chattanooga."

"General, right or wrong is of little consequence. We can only make decisions on the information we are given. We are both committed to the same goal, to defeat the Southern rebellion."

Rosecran blushes some, and says, "Thank you General Thomas, that is very generous, of you. Now, if you would give me your opinion about our future handling of the situation against General Bragg."

Thomas glances over the map, and studies the penciled lines and circles jotted across the map. Thomas drags a finger down a line to the Brotherton Farm and over to the Poe Field, and then on to the Kelly Field clearing.

Rubbing his gray beard Thomas says, "Presently, a gap in our line, maybe a span of 300 yards exist between Brotherton and Poe fields. General Brannan is taking care of that tonight.

Rosecran interrupts, "We have another similar problem, where a quarter of mile wide gap exist, between your right and Crittenden's left.

Thomas's eyes widen with that bit of startling news. "If the enemy, was ever to discover this, our chips are spent," Thomas says.

Rosecran adds, "The solution is quite obvious, but that in lies the trouble. If I move Crittenden north to fix it, I'll weaken our right flank."

Thomas quietly thinks this over for a minute, but is hesitant to give his opinion, before he makes a point. "This is what happens when an Army ceases to be offensive, and becomes defensive. We start reacting to the situation, instead of controlling the situation. That is not to say, we no longer have a way out."

"I'm Listening" Rosecran queries.

General Garfield interrupts to say "why not move Van Cleve's division out of his reserve position and place him up on the line on Crittenden's left and put Davis's division on his right. That way the hole is plugged and our right isn't weakened.

Rosecran smiles at the suggestion and says "my trusted Chief of Staff, you have earned your pay this day."

Thomas says nothing. His silence is puzzling and stirs Rosecran to say "General Thomas what do you say? You agree or disagree?"

"I'm not sure he sighs, his idea is good only if you plan to remain on the defensive. If that is the case you might as well put your reserves to work."

Thomas taps on the map with his finger and says "I have two of my divisions here way out of place. Palmer's with Johnson's divisions are so far out they could conceivably get cut off. I have ordered Johnson to pull back to a ridge closer to our line. We could on the other hand, bend my left to the east by moving Brannan and Reynolds thus cupping our center, offering a better offensive position to envelop the enemy."

Rosecran gets a worried look on his face. He checks his pocket watch and says, "a night maneuver in these dense woods is too risky. Could get them all confused and scrambled. I think we should stay put for now."

"That certainly makes sense, we can expect an all out effort from Bragg tomorrow," Garfield says.

"I certainly hope so, so we can get on the offensive" Thompson adds.

CHAPTER 31

General Pat Cleburne's Division halts their march north, and makes camp behind General Liddell's and Cheatham's Divisions, just east of Winfrey and Brock farms at the far northern end of General Bragg's line.

General Liddell, waste little time to pay his old friend, General Cleburne a visit, to discuss a plan he has in mind. Both Generals, once classmates at West point, are once again mates in the struggle for the Southern Cause.

"Patrick, you're a God send! We have been bucking against the tide all day, and they just keep thwarting everything we throw at them. Now, with you and your fresh troops here, we can finally shove them into Hell, once and for all." Liddell said.

"I heard it's been real rough going." Cleburne says.

"It's been a slaughter, but now with your Division, we have the numbers to change that."

"Well General, after we get a little rest and something to eat, we'll make a show of it tomorrow."

"Pat I'm not thinking about tomorrow. I'm talking about tonight, before they get reinforced. We've got to do it this evening."

Cleburne, stunned at the suggestion to attack in the dark, says, "General, my men are not familiar with the ground in these woods. We would be a danger, not only to ourselves but to your men as well. Hell, you know the odds of a night operation coming to anything but grief."

Liddell frustrated by his friend's refusal to listen to reason, asked him to accompany him to a sight overlooking the enemies campsite.

Both the men, side by side on their horses, overlook the area where the Yankees campfires dot the distant landscape.

"Pat look at that. They've got a brigade dangling out there, like a ripe apple ready to be picked. All we have to do is take advantage of this opportunity before they realize their mistake."

Cleburne nods, but before he can get a word out, they hear some noises, made by horsemen riding up through the woods that gets their attention.

In the dim light General D.H. Hill rides up, with his staff, and says, "Gentlemen am I missing something of interest here on this ridge?"

Cleburne, who finds General Hill most intolerable, can't look at him when he politely greets the General.

Liddell on the other hand, sees a chance, and quickly seizes on the opportunity to sell General Hill his plan, realizing Cleburne will have to obey the General, regardless.

"General, out there is the enemy encampment. We've have fought them all day, and they've killed a good many of our fine men this day, and we have gained nothing for it. Now, I am convinced, we can exact our share of retribution, they shall never forget."

General Hill gazes toward the enemy's encampment off in the distance, and asked, Liddell, what he has in mind.

Cleburne sits silently on his horse listening to his friend, propose his idea to General Hill.

Liddell's words, were just words on Cleburne's ears, for his mind was already formulating what he should do next, since he knew, Hill would never turn down a chance to glorify himself. Had this plan have come from Bragg, Hill would have ranted and raved, at the very notion.

Liddell is suggesting that Cleburne's three Brigades lead the attack, while his and General Cheatham's brigades, follow behind in support, since their forces had been reduced considerably from the morning action.

General Hill, likes his plan, but thinks three Batteries, using canister, should be included to be ready for the possibility of a counter attack. The dark will conceal their locations. Hill then looks at Cleburne, and asked if he had something he wanted to add.

Cleburne, stared for a moment at General Hill, and then turned his gaze to Liddell, realizing that to argue would be useless. However he finally says, "General Hill, the plan is sensible enough, but in the dark, it borders on insanity.

Hill's face reddens, as he says, General Cleburne, you are an insubordinate son of a bitch. What I want to know from you is if your brigades are capable of leading this attack?"

"General, I'm sure my men are as good as any soldiers in the dark."

General Hill, offended by Cleburne's disrespectful tone, swiftly responds, "General Cleburne, your Division will step off at 7:30 tonight, and proceeds through General Liddell's and General Cheatham's lines to lead the attack. I would suggest you have very little time to prepare, so you best get riding."

Cleburne quickly salutes, turns his horse and gallops off through the trees.

Cleburne is convinced Hill is right about one thing, and that is he has little time to prepare.

Cleburne, smart and efficient, cuts short is oratory with his commanders, and simply orders General Lucius Polk, General Polk's nephew, to place his brigade on the right, and General S.A. Wood to take the center, with General Deshler on the left. After crossing through Liddell's, and Cheatham's lines, they are to attack to the west, through the dense wilderness in the dark.

Polk looks at his pocket watch, 7:30. He tells his aides to spread the word to step off and begin the attack.

All along the line, stretching over a mile, each man carefully watches where he steps to avoid fallen limbs, rocks, depressions, and tangling Briar bushes ripping at their already tattered clothing.

Right from the start, as Cleburne had suspected, his brigade in the center gets disorganized filing through Liddell's line. The cohesion between these five regiments in Wood's confederate brigade becomes disrupted as they lose sight of each other.

General Polk, on the other hand, has little trouble maintaining the unity between his regiments, due to fact, that he doesn't need to cross through Liddell's ranks.

On the far left General Deshler, makes good time, but he drifts towards the south, losing contact with General Wood's left.

On the Union side of the line, General Baird's two brigades travel east through the woods to join up with General Johnson's Division as ordered by General Thomas.

Colonel Scribner leading the brigade on the left of General Starkweather makes the decision to halt for the night with dark approaching.

General Starkweather concurs, and also pitches camp, off Scribner's right.

Both brigades are camped only a couple hundred yards in the rear of Johnson's left flank.

Neither Commander fears a night attack, so they only post a picket line not bothering to post a skirmish line.

Out in the dark forest General Polk is stalking toward the Federals side door, advancing faster than the other brigades in Cleburne's attack force. He lies low when he reaches his jump off point waiting for the sound of musketry to come from the center of Cleburne's line.

He hasn't long to wait when the sounds of battle reach his ears.

Polk anxious to get on with the attack doesn't waste a second, spurring his regiments towards General Baird's unsuspecting Division, enjoying some much needed rest.

Polk's five regiments, pour in headlong out of the dark, firing a lethal volley into the startled brigade.

General Johnson has as yet to follow General Thomas's order to move his Division away from the Winfrey Field, and back to a commanding ridge deep in the woods. Johnson is about to learn a lesson first hand, why he should have heeded his Corp Commanders order sooner.

The attack at the center of Johnson's Division begins with only one of the regiments from General S.A. Wood's Confederate Brigade, storming over the section of the fence bordering Winfrey's Field held by Colonel Baldwin's brigade.

The dark camp sight, lit up by the many gun muzzle flashes created by the frantic soldiers who blaze away at anything that makes a noise.

Men of both sides scramble to reload as quickly as they can before they succumb to the bayonet.

Screams, from the wounded are heard over the din of the musket blasts and the angry shouts from the anxious men locked in to hand to hand combat.

Baldwin's union regiments worn to the nub, from the strenuous combat they've faced since early morning, are fighting on adrenalin alone against the fresh troops belonging Cleburne's Division.

All the rest of Cleburne's regiments, have yet to enter into the fray are slow to reach the Union defenses. The one lone Rebel regiment, the 45th Alabama continues to fight on gallantly, until they're overwhelmed and are forced back into friendly fire coming out the dark, in their rear.

These unfortunate Confederates aren't the only soldiers dieing from friendly fire.

Starkweather's union regiments also become confused in the dark from muzzles flashes off to their left. Thinking they may have been flanked, they mistakenly fire on one of the regiments in Scribner's brigade, killing some and wounding many.

Colonel Baldwin, caught up in the excitement of the close combat in the dark, insanely rides out in front of his line in a frenzied effort to lead his men on a counter attack. Baldwin is quickly blasted out of his saddle by a hail of bullets from the Confederate guns, instantly killing the Colonel and his horse.

Cleburne's left wing, lead by General Deshler, strays off track to the southwest of his intended path, which by luck will have it, places his brigade at the Unions back door, causing panic to spread like wildfire through Johnson's ranks, adding confusion and causing still more friendly fire casualties.

Johnson's command becomes weakened, and breaks at the seams as more Confederate regiments press in.

Time is literally running out for many of the men in Blue on the Winfrey field. But time is also running short for many of the men in Gray.

General Preston Smith, leading his brigade of Tennesseans, has but a short time left as well, when a shot out of the dark knocks him from his saddle. The wild shot passes through his gold pocket watch, and slices through his chest and into his heart. His loyal Tennessee boys, undaunted by his death, drive on, driving into the Federals in unbounded savagery, slaughtering the stubborn Yanks in their path and capturing scores of others.

The Rebels swarm in on both of Johnson's flanks, as well as overwhelming his center, and tearing into his rear.

The Division buckles under the strain. Johnson's stricken men run amuck, out of their minds with fear.

Cleburne, satisfied of his Division's accomplishments in the dark, decides not to pursue the retreating Yankees for now. Thinking he shouldn't press his luck, believing using caution, rather than testing the courage of a fool. It's hard to fight what he can't see, and he certainly can't see if the Federals have reserves on the way to retaliate.

The unspeakable mayhem slowly subsides in the evening mist.

But labor is not lost for General Johnson as he desperately works to find and reorganize what's left of his Division, on top of the ridge General Thomas had ordered him to occupy hours earlier.

Cleburne's troops stop to reorganize as well, a few hundred yards west of Winfrey field, pitching their bedrolls on the same ground gained in amongst the slain, now resting peaceably for all eternity.

CHAPTER 32

The hostilities have ceased for the night, but the planning activities for both the Union and Southern Headquarters are a buzz with activity.

General Polk meets with General Bragg to discuss a plan for the final destruction of Rosecran's Army of the Cumberland.

Bragg plans to simplify his chain of command, in hopes of creating a better coordination between his north and south flanks.

He places General Polk in command of his right wing, and General Longstreet in charge of his left.

Bragg stares intently from under his bushy dark eyebrows into Polk's eyes, and sternly states that there will be no excuse for not following his planned timetable for Sunday's attack the next day, with D.H. Hill leading the attack using Cleburne and Breckinridge as his openers.

"General Polk, this crusade begins at dawn tomorrow, and I expect it to begin on time" Bragg demands.

Polk the genteel sort not easily provoked by threats politely ignores Bragg's ugly demeanor, and mentions, "God will bless us with a victory, and remove this pestilence from our sacred homeland."

The 44th Mississippi is spending the night much the same as the night before. Several large fire pits, and many smaller cook fires dot the wooded campsite.

The 44th, having less than 300 men in their regiment, socially bond together through their smaller squads.

Today the 44th was spared the horrors of war thus the atmosphere in the encampment around the fire is of a lighter nature, needling one another, and joking about this and that, always the same night after night.

This night however isn't the same for many of the other encampments that weren't as lucky as the 44th, to be excluded from the killing, and maiming they endured today. These encampments are quiet with a somber feeling of remorse for the souls now missing, who only the night before were part of the humor.

Some of the survivors, victims of their gut wrenching memories from the ghastly sights they witnessed, are caused to search for an out of the way bush to puke in, or like some, stricken with tremors they can't stop. Still there are yet others capable of blocking out the ghastly pictures from their minds, and go on about their routines unaware that they too may someday become emotional cripples.

Pa Jones sits with his back to a tree cleaning his musket with loving care. Light from the fire cast a macabre shadow under his eyes accentuating the deep hollows in his cheeks.

Bay Flounders races past Pa heading for some privacy afforded in the dark woods.

Judd Archer lounging close by the fire next to Zach Singer, remarks, "looks like maybe Bay has them trots Sergeant Sawyer was warnings us about, you know about boiling our water and such."

Zach looks over and studies Judd for a second without saying anything, then turns to stare back at the fire, watching the flames dance over the burning wood.

Judd feeling a little unwelcome by the shun Zach gave him, gets up and moseys over to visit with Pa Jones.

Pa looks up at Judd while he continues to rub the musket and says "good evening boy, get your supper down okay tonight?"

"Yea, well actually no, don't feel much like eaten much. My stomach is kind of jumpy tonight. Probably getten what Bay's got.

"Nah, doubt it boy. Causin ifen ya had, you'd done be a walkin about like some bow legged old man. What'cha got boy ain't nutten but jitters, and they'll soon turn into the shivers before long."

Judd begins scratching like he's got itches all over, and says, " I think I got is a bad case of chiggers."

Pa chuckles, "aint no chiggers son, it's the fight tomorrow, everybody gets them their first time going into a fight. No shame in it though just the natural way of things."

Judd looks at Pa wide eyed, wondering if the man clearly sees through him and knew what he is thinking, and see the fear that's eating at his soul.

Pa continues, "Scared that be the reason boy. You aint sure yet how you gonna react to all the noise and such that'll be going on tomorrow, that's all. But don't you worry none cause tomorrow you'll be so scared your musket will slip in your hands, your heart will feel as if it's gonna jump clean out of your chest. You wont be able to remember at times if ya charged your musket or not, yea son aint nutten be a shame about none of that of either. Some never get over it. They get the jitters every time before the shooten starts. You can see it in their faces for sure. They get quiet and stare, or go around jabbering on and on about nothing. War is stupid, there aint no parades and cheering home folks. It's all about misery and horrible haunting happenings that don't want to leave the mind at peace. No boy aint nutten to be ashamed of when ya can't find peace of mind. The only peace you'll find around here is the kind that comes from God, and he's the only one that can give it to ya. I aint no preacher, but that's the gospel boy."

Judd staring out into the dark woods listening to Pa catches sight of Bay Flounder stumbling back in out of dark. His face is pale and expressionless. He looks Judd in the eye and says nothing as he passes.

Pa says "that boy is either sick or he's in the midst of a powerful struggle with them jitters."

Judd looks back at Pa sitting there slowly rubbing his musket, and says " Pa thanks for your time, I'll be a going back to my bedroll now, I suspect with all that's gonna be going on tomorrow I best get some rest, you have a good night Pa."

Pa responds "I'll see ya tomorrow son God be willin, and remember there aint no shame."

Judd turns and quietly walks away to his bedroll laid out on top of a pile of leaves he's learned to gather to soften the ground. He lies down and closes his eyes to mull over the things Pa had said. His mind drifts over this and that, finally the mention of God stirs his mind. It's been quite a while since he had thought about God, a long time, a long, long time.

CHAPTER 34

General Bragg's night is filled with organizing the many parts in his plan to continue the pressure on Rosecran the following morning.

Not long after General Polk departed for his own headquarters after conferring with General Bragg involving his role in Sunday's planned attack at dawn, when General James Longstreet walks through the door a little before midnight.

Weary from his long arduous train trip from Virginia that took days, he never the less is elated to be home on his native soil. Anxious to get on with his duties, given the fact he has a special interest to rid his homeland of the Yankee invaders.

Told of his roll, commanding the whole left of Bragg's southern wing, Longstreet sets about organizing the parts the leading Actors will play in this deadly Act.

On the other end of the stick, on the northern wing of the operation, the man responsible for honing the planned dawn attack has yet to meet with his star player.

D.H. Hill, who is to report to General Polk's headquarters for his instructions pertaining to his roll in the initial dawn attack, has not shown up.

Hill the narcissistic Corp commander is unable to find his way in the dark to Polk's headquarters. Twice he attempts to locate these headquarters but fails in both attempts, finally gives up and cashes in for the night.

Polk the genteel easy going Bishop decides, after he hasn't heard from General Hill, to send a courier with the battle plans and then calls it a night and retires to his bed.

The startling differences between Longstreet and Polk, makes their working relationship an accidental nightmare.

Longstreet would have personally gone searching for General Hill, and in all probability would have most likely fired him when he found him. Polk on the other hand went to bed. Either way it is of no wonder why Longstreet makes the comment that the only General he runs into that night who is looking forward to a victory the next day is General Hood. The same man he shared his experiences with at Gettysburg that July.

Hood is still recovering from wounds he received in that battle, but is still full of fight, and optimistic the Confederacy will prevail.

Across the great divide on the Union side changes are being scrutinized to sort out the confusion in the line caused by the daylong adjustments from trying to fend off the enemy.

General Thomas realizes he is on the defensive and has to accept that fact. Accustomed to finding weaknesses in the enemy's lines makes it easier for him to pinpoint his own vulnerabilities. The trouble however is the solution involves time and resources, neither of which is very plentiful. Thomas has convinced Rosecran at last evening's conference to send him additional reinforcements to beef up his left flank.

Thomas immediately drafts a message to his 2nd divisional commander General James Negley.

Negley up early this Sunday morning feeling a little rough has a cup of coffee with Colonel Sirwell his 3rd brigade commander. Warming by the fire they chat about yesterday and the possibilities of this and that that might come up.

A courier rides up out of the dark and delivers a message for Negley from Thomas. Negley reads the message then hands it to Sirwell. He then says "well Colonel we're on the move again today. Campaigning can wear a man thin. You better get your men up and fed. I'll get a hold of Colonel Stanley. Ah you can fall in behind him and follow him up the LaFayette road."

"General Sir isn't it strange there is no mention of who our relief is. If we get up and just leave with no relief, we're going to leave one hell of hole in our line for the Rebs to walk through."

"I'm sure that no doubt General Thomas has arranged for our replacement."

General Garfield chief of staff for Rosecran keeps the battle maps in the headquarters impeccably thorough and up to date. Even though Rosecran has this technology to direct troop dispositions from inside his headquarters he likes to check out things for himself in person. That way he is absolutely certain his directives are followed to the tee.

Rosecran decides to get out riding before dawn this Sunday morning checking on the integrity of his lines.

The dark horizon is fading when General Negley's first brigade under General Beatty takes to the LaFayette road for their trek north to join General Thomas's position at the north end of the Union line.

General Stanley has his 2nd brigade formed up and ready to move out when General Rosecran happens by and discovers to his surprise, Negleys men pulling out of the line. Rosecran is beside himself and demands from Negley the reasons behind this insanity. "Do you realize the hole you are leaving in my line Sir, and under what authority do you have to make such a blunder?"

General Negley doing his best to control his temper at this outburst in front of his staff, quickly hands Rosecran the message from Thomas, and says "I received the message just before dawn."

Rosecran tones down his demeanor as he reads over the message from General Thomas. "General Negley my apology. Stand by and hold this position for now until relieved."

Rosecran knows Thomas well enough to know that he has certainly made the necessary arrangements for Negley's relief, so where the hell is the relieving party?

The first place he goes looking is General McCooks camp, simply because he has two divisions presently held there in reserve. On his way to McCook's he meets up with General Thomas Wood, whose division is presently held in reserve and the nearest to Negley's division. Wood a tenacious commander is a good pick to replace Negley on the line. So Rosecran orders him to report to Negley, and the quicker the better. That problem solved, he now continues on with his investigation to find out just where and why the breakdown occurred.

An hour has passed since he discovered the slip up, and time has incensed his fury. He stomps into McCook's headquarter in a simmering mood and loudly demands to know what McCook knows about Negley's relief.

McCook taken back by his aggressive behavior tries to explain he knows nothing of a message from Thomas requesting any transfers. He searches through the messages on his desk finding nothing before he calls his Adjutant over to see if he knows anything about this. The Adjutant admits a message came for Generals Jefferson Davis and Sheridan late last night, and that he forwarded it on, figuring it was best not to wake McCook, since he hadn't slept for two days.

Rosecran's face reddens as he asked the Adjutant why he is yet to inform the General of this Communique.

"General we just learned a courier was mistakenly killed by one of our pickets last night.

I was trying to find out which courier so I would have all the information to inform the General. We have now learned it was the courier carrying the messages from General Thomas.

CHAPTER 35

The sun is reaching the tops of the tree line, as Negley, feeling sicker, impatiently waits for his relief to show. It's close to nine o'clock when General Wood finally arrives with his command.

"General Wood Sir, I'll move my men out of the way, I think you'll find the breastworks my men created to your liking. They worked like devils most of the night constructing that wall." "Thank you General, we will defend it with great care" Wood says.

Colonel Sirwell's brigade steps out on the road for their short march up the LaFayette road.

Private Long gripes to his pals John Davis and James Farr as they begin the march "You know we spent the better part of the night building that damn wall of logs and such, and now we gotta leave it to them Yokels in the XXI Corp. It just aint right you know. I'm either digging some shit ditches for others to crap in or building defenses for someone else to lie behind.

Farr feeds Long's aggravation "Hell brother Long it's a good thing we're moving now, cause it's better than watching you run off later." "James Farr speak for your own damn self, there aint nobody gonna run me off." Davis then says "Excepting a screaming Reb bearing down on ya."

Wood's two brigades file in behind Negely's column and take over the ramparts. Buell's brigade replaces Sirwell's brigade while Harker's brigade takes Stanley's place in the line, leaving one place in the line uncovered, so Wood borrows a brigade from Van Cleve to fill the space.

Up the road General Beatty is directed to take a position on the far left of Thomas's line. He's told he'll have to spread himself thin until the rest of his division arrives. Unhappy with this decision to hang his brigade out on a limb, he decides to place his two batteries at opposite ends of the position to help cover some of the ground he can't with the few men he has.

Beatty is no fool he has only four regiments and three quarters of a mile to defend. He quickly needs to come up with a plan he can execute if in the event he has to fall back. The clearing on the McDonald farm behind him offers absolutely no protection. The only possible direction would be the woods to the south, the same woods he traveled through this morning. But before he can make that decision he first wants to meet the brigade commander Colonel Joseph Dodge who is positioned next to him on the right. Beatty is satisfied he has done all he can do here so now he leaves to find Commander Dodge only a short ride away.

"I saw your outfit come through this morning, nice to have you for my new neighbor colonel", Dodge says as he greets him.

"I'm not sure what kind of a neighbor I'll be, I've got a lot of ground to cover with very few men I'm afraid."

"Well the bad news is the Rebs will know all about your strength soon enough." Beatty nods. "If I get overrun Colonel I plan to move my men here behind your line. So you could pass the word so your men won't mistaken us for Rebs. We will be the guys in blue."

"That suits me fine Dodge says, my line faces more to the north so I can pour enough lead into their flank to send them all to hell in a hurry. Actually if they were to follow you in behind me we could pinch them off at the neck."

"Clever, the old bait and take, very good Sir. Colonel Dodge, I feel much better after our talk, thank you."

"Good luck Colonel" Dodge says.

Beatty rides off to brief his regimental commanders feeling the need to hurry to make use of what little time he may have. The time is now 9:30 Sunday morning.

Colonel Dodge takes a moment to talk with General King whose brigade is dug in, in an orchard next to him on the right.

King tells him he is concerned about the condition of Colonel Scribner's brigade after the licking they took last night on the Winfrey

Field. "Hell we've all fed the "Beast" the last two days. I think the Rebs must be as tired as we are, maybe they'll take it easy today.

"I'm not so sure General, I think they're getting replacements from where I don't know, but there damn sure seems to be a hell of a lot of them," Dodge declares.

CHAPTER 36

Bragg damn near jumps out of his boots once again as the sun's pink rays fan out across the horizon and not a single sound is heard other than the morning chorus from the chirping birds.

Fuming he screams "Can't that damn Episcopal Bishop ever carry out a plan at the proper time, that son of a bitch is one of the laziest bastards in the whole Confederacy.

An orderly holds Braggs horse as he struggles to get his boot in the stirrup, adding to his agitation. The Major quickly comes to his rescue and gives him a hand. Once aboard, he slowly rides away awkwardly do to his age and ailments.

Polk is up and also becomes concerned when he hears nothing. He immediately heads for General Hill's headquarters. After riding less than a mile he comes upon General Hill holding court with some of his staff officers. Polk politely inquires why the attack hasn't begun.

General Hill rather curtly replies he just received the directive only minutes before and the attack would have to wait until his men finished their breakfast.

Polk though aghast by this insubordinate excuse, never the less doesn't press the issue and decides to leave it up to General Hill to proceed when ready.

The meeting isn't quite so sweet when Polk happens upon Bragg on the Alexander Bridge Road. Polk tries to convince the General there was a mix up in the communications last night and that he had spoken with Hill and everything was straightened out. He adds the attack should begin within the hour.

Bragg not happy with this flimsy excuse blurts out "I should have the bunch of you put in chains for the deliberate disobedience to orders. That would be what I should do, but in the end what good would it do, Jeff Davis would just send more lawyers and preachers. Thank the Lord I've got Longstreet to command my left wing." He then lowers his heavy brow and threatens "this battle has been delayed all it's going to be delayed. Now you ride back and get it started right now."

Bragg turns his horse and bounces away on the poor horse.

Polk watches him ride off and says "If that man ever lived before I'm sure he sat at the foot of the Cross with dice in one hand and the Robe in the other."

The enterprising General Longstreet has carefully prepared his planned attack by placing his pieces on the board precisely where they will closely support one another arranged in a manner similar to a set of waves breaking on the shore. The front ranks are strengthened by the second wave and the second wave is followed by the third. The best of fortifications will be hard pressed to withstand the tide of men crashing down upon them.

Longstreet wants his best division to lead the attack and he feels Hood's old division now under Evander Law is just that division.

Longstreet campaigned with General Hood at Gettysburg when Hood's division made a reputation by storming up the slopes of "Little Round Top" thrice under a withering fire against all odds, showing no yellow in their blood only red kind pooled in the rocks.

By now it has become apparent to Longstreet the Federals are shoring up their left with more and more troops moving in that direction, all told by the dust clouds stirred up due to the hot dry weather.

The failed attempts by Bragg the last two days may after all paid dividends.

Longstreet seizes upon this error in judgment and makes plans to take full advantage of it.

He has to wait for Polk to make the first move against the Federal left to get them to take their eyes off of their right flank. Then the time will be right to slam his fist into their southern reaches followed up with an uppercut that will buckle their knees causing their right to fold like a broken twig.

Lieutenant Bishop wearing his finest gray dress coat stands in front of his platoon conferring with Sergeant Sawyer. His men formed up behind him, stand at ease waiting for the word from Longstreet to attack. Thousands of other men just like them are lined up in a battle formation that stretches out for more than a mile.

Bishop seems a bit nervous scratching the ground with his sword and knocking weeds about with the tip.

Sergeant sawyer on the other hand appears to be quite calm; spitting ever now and then a swath of tobacco juice far from the Lieutenant.

Judd Archer scared and anxious about what lies ahead, feels a whole lot better than he did last night thanks to his talk with Pa Jones.

Now however standing in line next to Bay Flounders, Judd feels half sick because Bay smells so bad. He permeates of vomit and other foul smells. Zack Singer standing on the other side of Bay complains "Damn it Bay you need to wash yourself, you smell worse than a putrifying old body. You must have shit yore trousers and done vomited all over yoreself.

Bay's pale face flushes, and then he suddenly breaks out of the rank and takes off running back through the woods. Sergeant Sawyer hollers out for Bay to stop, but Bay pays him no attention and keeps on running.

"Let him go Sergeant Zack yells, "hell the stench in these here woods is stink enough with all them bloaten bodies laying about."

Sergeant Sawyer walks up to Zack and sniffs him and says "You aint smelling so good yourself private, so how about shutten that big mouth of yours while your in the ranks." Sawyer walks back over to Lt. Bishop to take his place and declares "Bay aint gonna be no help no how, just get himself killed." Bishop responds, "Sergeant I can't permit my men to come and go as they please."

"Yes sir Lieutenant." Sawyer spins on his heels and looks up and down the rank. "Judd Archer, fall out and go find Bay and take him to the surgeons, then get back here you hear."

"Private Archer I'll see you here for a minute" orders Bishop. The Lieutenant takes a scrap of paper and pens a note authorizing Judd's absence in case he gets questioned. He hands him the paper and says, "find him and then get back and don't linger."

Judd stuffs the paper in his pocket, salutes and takes off running after Bay. He runs only a short distance and then slows to a walk to catch his breath. After crossing a narrow wagon road he smells a foul smell coming from somewhere near by. He stops to look around and then notices a shallow crater burnt in the weeds. There several bodies bloated and swarming with large black flies crawling over them lie in and around the hole. Their features so grotesquely swollen they hardly look human anymore. The odor is so strong Judd begins to wretch, losing what little breakfast he had gotten down this morning.

Suddenly Judd hears someone say "Pretty aint it."

Judd wipes his mouth and gets up off his knees to see where the voice came from.

Sitting on the ground leaning back against a tree is Bay Flounders. The redness around his eyes contrasting with his pallor complexion gives him a ghostly appearance.

"Bay, how come you done and lit out like that" Judd asked? The Lieutenant has done and sent me after you. Why did you go and run off like that Bay?"

Bay kind of wheezes when he says "it aint causen I'm scared like they think. I need to get back to that creek I gotta clean up myself, if I can only make it there. Can you help me Judd? I'd help you. Judd I don't want to die like this."

"Bay the Sergeant told me to take you to the surgeons."

Bay thumps the back of his head against the tree and pleads "Don't you see all I want is to clean myself up in the creek Judd, so I can then fight. I don't need no surgeon, all I want is some help so I can reach that damn creek; it aint that far off. Bay struggles to get to his feet, he staggers a bit and begins to fall. Judd quickly grabs him and holds him steady. Bay whimpers, "Judd I shit myself, oh God I hate it, all I do is vomit and shit and vomit again. I gotta get to the creek so I can wash up."

"Sure Bay I'll get you to the creek you just lean on me and we'll get you there. Bay you seem awful hot, maybe you done and got the fever."

They walk only a few paces when Bay quits using his legs and slumps in Judd's arms. Judd lays him down gently and holds his head under his arm. Bay whispers, "I don't wanna die smellen like I do. You'll get me to the creek?" His voice trails off as his body relaxes and his breathing becomes labored. Judd fumbles with his canteen to get the cap off. He throws the cap down and lifts Bay's head to give him a drink. His mouth drops open his head is heavy and lifeless, his chest is no longer heaving. His redden eyes glaze over. Judd lays Bay's head down and stands up looking down at his graying face, thinking how Bay had survived all those battles, and now the only thing that scared him most was dieing in his filthy condition.

Judd looks around realizing he can do nothing for Bay now. He can't lift the lifeless body and drag it hundreds of yards to the creek. Besides what good would it do now?

Off in the distance he hears the muffled booming of cannons and the faint screams of men yelling.

CHAPTER 37

General Breckenridge's division is selected to begin the assault against the Union left. His three brigades form up using the South's traditional single line formation.

General Daniel Adam a Georgia native leads his brigade to initiate Bragg's battle plan followed by General Stovall's brigade in the center and General Helm's on the left.

They use the landscape to conceal their presence the land isn't flat or level it's constructed of hills and dales that's covered by dense wilderness of both large and small trees carpeted with thick underbrush.

Like islands, cleared farm fields sit in the middle of this wooded rolling terrain, which are serviced by narrow crude wagon roads.

This is the stage that the last Act of Bragg's Opera is to be played on.

Adams brigade first appears from out of the dense forest like a sudden storm on the unprepared regiments along the Union's extreme left.

Adam's Louisiana boys easily sweep away half of Beatty's brigade on the far left. The ones that aren't killed or captured scatter to the west across the McDonald farm field running for their lives.

General Stovall's brigade in the middle enjoys a quick rout of the 104th Illinois regiment, leaving only the 15th Kentucky to face the onslaught of two fellow Kentucky regiments fighting for the Confederacy. The 15th at a two to one disadvantage has to back away and escape with the 104th retreating into the woods on the west side of the LaFayette road behind the Union flank held by the three brigades of Dodge, King, and Scribner.

Breckenridge's left is feeling the effects of running up against Baird's breastworks.

General Helm's left three Confederate regiments receive a lethal dose of lead in their attempt to charge into the strongly defended line.

The Southern pride runs deep and causes men to make fatal choices and ignore common sense.

The hollow lead projectile instantly makes messes of anything it comes into contact with.

A large gap yawns open between Stovall's brigade and Helm's.

Adam and Stovall gather together their scattered victorious soldiers to get their breath and reform their line for a push south and finish off the retreating Yankees.

"Charge" is the shout that reverberates through the woods as they race forward through the woods yelling and screaming like crazed demons chasing after the retreating elements of Beatty's brigade.

Colonel Stanley and his 2nd brigade marching north up the LaFayette road to join Beatty is but a short jaunt away from where Beatty is stubbornly attempting to slow down the onslaught of Rebs by firing as he retreats.

Stanley orders his Union brigade forward on the run.

Still another Union brigade hurries up the road to help fortify the Union left is Colonel Van Derveer closing fast on the heels of Stanley's brigade.

In the mean time Helm's Confederates are driven back from their assault against the north corner of the Union line reducing their ranks considerably. Once again the old Southern pride rules as they regroup and take off to achieve their glorious defeat over their Northern invaders.

General Helm heroically leading his men on when suddenly his stomach is torn from his body by Yankee lead that sends him tumbling to the ground for the last time.

Neither Stovall nor Adam is aware of what is happening to Helm's brigade. Both continue on with their rampage through the woods until their brigade runs into the added firepower thrown their way with Stanley's arrival on the field.

Stovall feels the wrath of Van Derveer's brigade also, that gives him a taste of what is coming his way. Things really get sideways for Stovall when Dodge and Scribner's second line of defense does an about face and unloads a devastating broadside against his left flank.

General Adam damn near has his arm blown off that throws him from his saddle. Beatty and Stanley then counter charge with a terrifying bayonet attack that effectively changes the Rebels attitude, for they want no part of the Unions cold steel. The tables have turned on them when they no longer have the upper hand over the Federals overwhelming numbers.

The stunning reversal in the Yanks fortune doesn't deter General Thomas from pleading with Rosecran for additional reinforcements to further strengthen his left.

If things weren't going bad enough for Bragg with the late start allowing the Yankees time to beef up their defenses and then the added disappointment of watching General Breckenridge's advance repulsed on the right, and now General Cleburne's division on Breckenridge's left isn't doing any better. The Confederates are finding the Yankee breastworks are hazardous to their health. And worse yet they don't know how to overcome the problem.

Cleburne's third brigade, General Deshler's Texans haven't had the chance to either succeed or fail because there is no room for them to advance.

General A.P. Stewart's division belonging to General Longstreet's Corp have got themselves out of position and are north of the Confederate center where they should have been.

This unscripted comedy of errors gets more confused and frustrating for Longstreet when he learns Bragg has become impatient and sent orders to all front line commanders to attack at once without delay.

Longstreet quickly sends word to all his commanders countermanding the order, all except Stewart who doesn't receive the countermand in time. Stewart was meeting with General Cleburne discussing the need for Stewart to begin his attack to help take the heat off of Cleburne's left that is getting nowhere against Baird's line, when Braggs order arrives telling everyone to get engaged.

Stewart orders his brigade commanders General Bate and General Brown to launch an attack across the Poe Field that was the scene of plenty of blood letting the day before.

The bent configuration of Brannan's Union line accidentally affords him the benefit of applying a crossfire pattern for anyone foolish enough to enter his killing zone in the open field.

General Brown on the right is the first to step out. The minute he clears the tree line and starts across the open field the Union line behind their log breastwork opens up with a field of fire that includes Grapeshot from their artillery with also a high volume of musketry.

General Bate charges their men across the northern half of the field receiving a full dose of the Yankee medicine.

The Poe field is thus receiving a good measure of Southern home grown fertilizer this September day, compliments of General Bragg. With no where to run to escape the carnage the lucky survivors fall on their bellies and crawl back out of the hell they walked into.

Up the road General Deshler and his tough Texans now have room to wade in and show how it should be done. Never had they assaulted a strongly entrenched enemy before, so they courageously charge forth and quickly learn a very hard lesson. Fortunately for them they found a ridge they could lie behind to protect them and still maintain contact with the enemy until they have to fall back for ammunition.

Cleburne witnessing the frivolous blood letting, that is decimating his command, calls for a halt to all advances.

Without the proper positioning for the artillery to blast the breast-works, a frontal assault is doomed to fail.

Cleburne's decision was too late to save one of his brigade command-ers, General Deshler who literally lost his heart from a cannon ball.

Many other lives could have been spared on both sides if Power, Valor, Greed and Stubborn Pride all the necessary ingredients to produce the "Monster" that feeds on soldiers no matter the color of the uniform.

General William Walker, commander of General Bragg's Reserve Corp, rides up to confer with General D.H. Hill who has the respon-sibility to crush the Yankee left. Walker's Corp is responsible to aid or strengthen the first line of Offense when called upon.

General Walker like so many of his fellow officers has a total disdain for D.H. Hill. But he feels the need to confront him, so Walker pulls his horse up directly in front of Hill and minces no words when he says

"General Hill I feel it is advisable to tell you Sir to wait no longer to utilize my reserves. We need to bolster the entire line before it gets to damn weak to do so."

A scowl forms across Hill's face because of the audacity Walker uses to approach him this way. With a tone flavored with the most sour vinegar Hill replies, "General Walker when you have the where with all to advise me, then and only then will I listen to anything you have to say. Until your command is blessed with General Gist appearance I will not commit one man from your reserve Corp. So you go back and await further orders from me."

The exasperated Walker retorts "Gist, hell I've got Ector, Wilson and Lidell's divisions, plus Govan's and Wathall's brigades sitting idle. Walker abruptly backs his horse up and says, "if we lose here, the shame will be on your head." With that said he spurs his horse and gallops off.

Foreboding news is delivered to General Hill shortly after General Walker's departure. Breckenridge and Cleburne have both been unable to break the Union line and are driven back.

Hill has to swallow his pride and sends orders to Walker to release his reserves at once. Fortunately for Hill, General Gist has just arrived with his brigade and takes command of Ector's division as well. Gist new to the battle here knows absolutely nothing of the enemy's strength. He only knows he has the opportunity to achieve glory and enhance his name in the newspapers. To be a part of the force that throws out the hated Yankee invaders from the Heart of the South, his beloved South, to help preserve their way of life is worth dieing for and to leave a legacy for generations to come to read about. A South with her large cotton plantations and endless fields of nuts of all kind, is not polluted with foreigners and their strange ideals that have turned the North against the South. The only foreigners here are the Blacks from Africa and the Caribbean Islands that have never been included in Southern society. They are only used for their muscle to keep the plantations running profitably, like boilers in a locomotive. And now these damn Yankees want to come and change all of that, more than a century's way of life.

General Walker lays out the battle plan for Gist, the famous "States Rights" activist, and says "General so far we haven't been able to crack the Union line, and I'm not so sure it can be done. We've wasted a lot of fine boys so far trying to do just that. Their line is dug in tighter than a Boll Weevil."

"General Walker we will crush the bastards and bring you Rosecran for a gift, you just tell me where the hell they are Sir."

CHAPTER 38

General George Thomas has been up against it all morning. His line has done more than any commander could ask. Yesterday and into last night they have fought off everything Bragg has thrown at them. They've made mistakes and plenty of them, but they still were able to regroup and preserve the lines integrity. Thus far Thomas has been supplied all the men needed to overcome the persistent attacks from Bragg.

Thomas would like to have the rest of Brannan's division to add more men on the northern corner of his line where a good deal of the Confederates effort has taken place thus far and where he figures they will certainly continue to attack again.

Brannan spread out behind Poe Field has just denied A.P. Stewart's attempt and has successfully pushed him back on his heels. He has hardly had time to reload when he receives the order to move north. Brannan not one to deliberately disobey an order, has reservations and thinks that Thomas may not be aware of the threat to Poe Field.

General Reynolds 4th division is too thin to cover the field alone.

Brannan sends word to Rosecran that Reynolds will need some help to cover the field once he leaves.

Brannan and Reynolds put their heads together to weigh the possibilities and consequences of leaving the area at this time. The Confederates as active as they had been recently on his front Brannan figures he should wait and hold tight to make certain Thomas has the right impression or at least until he is properly relieved.

In the mean time Rosecran gets Brannan's message and must make the decision with whom to replace him with. He decides to pull General

Thomas Wood's division out of the line covering Brotherton Field and have him join Reynolds on Poe Field.

All this many unit transfers and no explanations, cause the commanders to question the validity of such orders, and Wood is no different when he takes this order to his Corp commander General Alexander McCook for an opinion. McCook tells him he has no choice but to obey the order immediately.

Wood has three brigades in his division and informs Colonel Barnes to start his brigade on the road followed by Colonel Harker's brigade. After all nothing has happened along their front since yesterday afternoon and there is no indication the rebels are about to renew the fight on the southern sector.

But like a hidden snake in the grass Longstreet is coiled and ready to strike, playing his cards like a master thief.

He is almost discovered though when a Union regimental commander from Buell's brigade decides on his own initiative to march his men across Brotherton Field and into the eastern woods.

Buell commanding the third brigade in Wood's division isn't convinced this sector is passé. He complains, "I fear we are taking the bait and falling prey to their tricks. Out there in those woods a formidable enemy waits for us to do something fool hearty. I can smell the dirty bastards like a wild animal sniffs danger."

Colonel Bartleson on his adventure through the woods at the head of his regiment runs into plenty of evidence when he walks into a skirmish line along Longstreet's front.

Like a mouse coming face to face with the proverbial cat, the scene is one of panic and mayhem.

The egregious decision by Colonel Bartleson has left half his men lost in the woods either dead or captured.

Near by in the same woods, Judd Archer walks slowly back through woods alone and sad over Bay Flounder's death. He suddenly is jolted out of his depression by the noises from the rattle of musketry a little ways off in the distance that causes him to hurry his pace. Naturally hesitant to place himself in mortal danger, he still is anxious to get his chance to be involved in a real battle.

Judd is stopped when he tries to run past a line of troops. A Major then demands an explanation for his lone presence.

Judd fumbles through his pockets searching for the pass Lt. Bishop had given him. Afraid maybe he could have dropped it running through the woods he desperately searches through his pants.

The Major, suspecting he may have deserted says "Private if you didn't know it you are running in the wrong direction, if you are gonna steal away, you ought to at least start in the right direction." As the Major is laughing at him, Judd finally finds the pass in his shirt pocket and hands it to the officer. The Major reads the message and hands it back to Judd and says "Boy I guess you know where you are headed but you better be more careful with this pass or you could end up dead at the hands of the wrong army. Now get along with you."

Judd takes off running once again until he reaches the platoon still waiting for the word to move out.

Gasping for air, he takes his place in the line.

Sergeant Sawyer turns around to ask "Private Archer, you think you should report with some news about your mission?"

"Yes Sergeant. Bay Founders is dead Sergeant. He died back yonder a ways in the woods." Lt. Bishop ask, "What was the cause of death, Private?"

"He died in my arms Sir. He was trying to reach the creek to wash up." Judd looks to his left and stares at Zach and adds "He was awful sick and didn't want to die stinking the way he did, that is why he ran off."

Pa Jones speaks up "God will bless poor Bay Flounders, lets hope he doesn't need to bless the rest of us this day."

A silence falls over the platoon until Sergeant Sawyer barks "Ok, you've made your peace, don't forget you are in ranks, and if you want to ponder about something, think about getting mean, cause when we step out I want to hear a fearful shout you hear. We gotta send those Yankee bastards to hell where they belong. So get good and mad boys!"

A rider rides up to the Colonel standing not far away on a hill behind them. He says something to the Colonel then rides off. The Major, standing next to the colonel pulls his revolver from his holster raises the pistol above his head and fires two shots. The signal they had been waiting so long to hear.

Lt. Bishop raises his saber and thrust it forward. The shrill coming from the many throats diminishes the anxiety and fear that plagued their hearts giving them the courage to face the consequence of death.

Judd walking in line next to Zach yelling at the top of his lungs feels an emotion he has never experienced before. He is now a part of something great, something historical. This is the happiest, thrilling moment of his young life.

Suddenly a thought flashes across his mind that is explosive; he forgot to load his musket. Here he is charging into the enemy for the first time with an empty musket.

They come to the edge of the woods and there, before them lays open ground.

Lt. Bishop pauses to let the line dress up. Judd quickly pulls his ramrod, and reaches for his powder and mini ball. He shoves the powder down and drops the ball in the barrel and starts pounding it down when Zach says "Judd you know what the hell you are doing? You double charge that damn musket fool, and you'll blow yourself away and me too probably."

"No I won't Zach, I didn't charge it before we left, I forgot too."

Zach stares in disbelief and says "You was coming to this damn shooten match without a ball in the barrel boy? Judd you stay close to me and I'll get you through this."

There is the sign of a battle in the distance by the white smoke drifting above the trees. Boys and men are dieing up there. Some mothers sons never to be seen again.

What causes this thirst for another man's blood? Judd's mind is confused like never before while he waits for the order that will launch him to a place he has never experienced, killing another man.

How did it come to this, it wasn't suppose to be like this. The thought of going to war was to be glorious, conquering the foe, overcoming the enemy. Proud of his bravery achieved in the din of battle against shot and shell, with the bands playing, and drums beating.

It suddenly dawns on him he doesn't belong here. Watching Bay die in his arms like that and he definitely doesn't want to kill anyone. But he is trapped, trapped in a web of his own making, cast by men who aren't even here.

Lt. Bishop raises his saber high over his head the sun's rays glimmering off the blade.

Like a baby pulled from the womb, he is thrust into a world he knows nothing of, a chaotic world fraught with paralyzing fear. His inner soul begs for God to rescue him and take him away from this horrific nightmare.

Out of the dense woods he steps onto a cleared cornfield along with a regiment of screaming hellions.

The sun is so bright Judd covers his eyes as best he can. Somehow he draws the courage to move and keep moving.

CHAPTER 39

Colonel Buell's brigade the last to leave on General Wood's trek north fails to keep up. Two of his regiments get separated from the main body because they have to cover the slower paced battery trying to roll their heavy cannons over the rough difficult terrain.

All the action that is taking place along General Thomas's front on his northern sector has lured the Yankees into sending men away from the southern half. A trap Lonstreet set up beautifully, and Rosecran took the bait hook, line and sinker.

Rosecran's troubles are just beginning coupled with the fact that General McCook has pitifully been incapable to grasp the urgency of the situation.

The removal of General Wood's division has left a wide gap in the line undefended. The portion of the Union line off of Brotherton Field is where General Jefferson Davis and his two battered brigades have been assigned to defend.

North several hundred yards out of the east woods bordering Poe Field thousands of yelling demons emerge screaming for blood in front of the Yankee line along the Poe Field, south of the Brotherton Field.

Colonel Brannan's two brigades under Colonels Connelly and Beatty are the first Union regiments to feel the pain of Longstreet's onslaught.

The fragmented regiments in Buells brigade are completely unprepared to counter the onslaught. Caught with their pants down they desperately try to do what little they can against the overwhelming force.

Many of the Southern commanders experience quick successes, but some are finding the Federals a rough bunch to conquer.

General McNair's Southern brigade, a part of Bushrod Johnson's division is getting mauled at the breastworks in front of Colonels Beatty and Connell's tough defenders.

Falling like flies McNair's rebels are swallowing some of the same medicine A.P. Stewart's men swallowed earlier. McNair is forced to fall back and gather what is left to regroup and try again.

Further south the shoe is on a different foot. Colonel Fulton's Tennessee boys are making easy hay of it, sweeping aside the regiments guarding Buell's artillery that leaves the right flank of General Brannan open for the taking.

Colonel Cyrus Sugg raiding off to the left of McNair is in a good position to topple that flank, shredding the unprotected Federals weakened from the previous day's bout. It doesn't take long before Brannan's division crumbles piecemeal, eroding rapidly.

The stalwart breastworks that once had provided impregnable cover are now indefensible on the flank. The Yanks do their best against the swarming force as they are overrun. The battle gets close up and personal. The Yanks fighting with everything at hand don't survive long against the overwhelming numbers thrown at them.

McNair now has free access to bridge across the breastworks, to exact payment for his fallen comrades, stepping over those very losses sprawled over the ground to his front.

Colonel Croxton quickly reacts with what little time he has to face around two Kentucky regiments to meet head on Colonel Henry Benning's Georgians seeking revenge for their disastrous collision with Colonel Wilder's Spencer repeating rifles the day before.

South of the Brotherton Field in the woods east of the Dyer farm, Colonel Sugg tires of his chase to snag Brannan's retreating division. He turns to take on another Yankee competitor, General Jefferson Davis and his Illinois division with only two whittled down brigades with less than thousand men.

McCook makes an egregious decision sending these few men into the line without first determining what the situation is.

Davis has Sugg on his left and a new threat from General Hindman closing fast from the southeast to his right.

Davis's small division fights bravely, temporarily holding off Texans, Tennessee, and Alabamans. But outnumbered by five thousand muskets they will be fodder for their foe if they don't get the hell out of there.

McCook needs more men fast so he races off to get General Sheridan down to help Davis. While Sheridan is moving to engage the enemy, the future for the Federals on Poe field is getting dimmer.

The thick smoke from burning trees mixed with the black powder smoke squeezes the lungs and stings the eyes. The stench of decaying flesh is inescapable.

Men are desperately fighting to survive while others are just as desperately trying to make sure they don't.

The handsome Colonel Benning standing tall in his stirrups hollers for his Georgians to "charge and take the Yankees by the throat." They take off in a wild rage running hell bent against a storm of musket balls tearing through the air. Colonel Benning cartwheels out of his saddle when his horse's leg is torn off by cannon shot. His counter part isn't so lucky. Colonel Croxton goes down crippled by a mini ball that tears into his leg.

The 10th and the 74th Indiana regiments are swiftly stripped of their commanding officers but are not totally left leaderless.

Lt. Colonel Marsh Taylor steps in and takes charge of the brigade. All fired up and full of fight he immediately orders a bayonet charge right into the heart of Benning's charging Georgians. Insane as that may sound, for reasons only God would understand, the couple hundred men stand up and fix bayonets. Lt. Orville Chamberlain his saber in one hand and a pistol in the other with Sergeant Hoeppner close by his side leads the 74th along side the 10th and wades into the startled Georgians. Sergeant Hoeppner draws energy from the young Lieutenant who is slashing and firing his pistol at every gray clad soldier that gets in his way. Hoeppner is just as busy busting heads with the butt of his musket and running many through with his bayonet that his rifle becomes slick and sticky with the blood of his victims. The audacity of this unbelievable charge turns the tide and Benning's men scatter for their lives. Colonel Benning thinking all of his men must have been killed in the wild confusion, temporarily loses his mind and wonders around despondent making no sense.

The bold charge by the two Indiana regiments runs out of steam eventually when the high pitch of emotion subsides. Even for this young impetuous officer the lives of his men have now become forever a part of him. He knows their lives will depend on his ability to react swiftly to any unexpected threat.

Sergeant Hoeppner still panting from the vigorous combat notices and points out a rather large body of Rebels crossing the Dyer farm off to the west, with some others to the south to Lt. Chamberlain. "Sir we need to let Colonel Taylor know about them Rebs over there, I'm sure he can't see them from where he is."

Chamberlain tries to estimate the size and the distance of the enemy force through the thick haze of smoke. "Sergeant, send a runner to inform the Colonel that a brigade size enemy formation is approaching. Get the men gathered and formed up I want to close up on the 10th as soon as possible.

The boys have fought a good fight and we need to give them the best chance to fight another, but some of them will have to stay here and cover our move. Sergeant I hate to ask you but I need you to lead a skirmish line."

Chamberlain grabs his arm with a very serious expression in his eyes to say, "don't waste them, shoot only if you have to. When I get back with the 10th I'll send for you.

Sergeant Hoeppner sensing his sincere concern smiles and says, "you won't have to worry Lieutenant I'll take care they get back in fighting fiddle shape."

Hoeppner goes about barking orders as he hurries around to gather up the scattered men and select the ones he'll need for the skirmish line.

It doesn't take long to get the men reorganized once again. Fear has away of getting a man's attention faster than threats or reasonable explanations.

Lt. Chamberlain marches away with what is left of the regiment, as Sgt. Hoeppner and his men march off to the west a short distance before spreading out some ten yards apart in the tree line bordering on the Dyer field. Hoeppner selects a position that affords him a bird's eye view of the whole field but also concealing him from the probing eyes of men in the field.

Hoeppner watches as a Confederate General slowly leads a brigade through the field. Unbeknown to him this General is Jerome Robertson, who like General Longstreet, is on loan from the Army of Northern Virginia. His brigade of Texans have so far missed the fight today but are itching for their share of blood to gain atonement for Gettysburg that is still very fresh on their minds. Captain Cleveland leading the Confederate right flank loses sight of the other brigades in the dense woods. However he can see off to his right in the distance a disorganized horde of Confederate soldiers running in the opposite direction.

Captain Cleveland alarmed by the sight becomes alarmed that something has gone wrong to his front. He can't see any evidence that the other regiments have fallen back but he can't be sure. He decides to fall back a couple hundred yards to evaluate his situation. This inadvertent decision may have saved more lives than he will ever know, by avoiding Sgt. Hoeppner's hidden skirmish line.

In the meantime Sgt. Hoeppner receives word from Lt. Chamberlain to rejoin the regiment that is moving north with the 10th. Hoeppner feels however he needs to slow down the approach of the Rebel force, so he orders the men to fire three volleys and then they will quietly but quickly retire back into the forest.

His plan works like a charm, the first volley causes the Rebels to drop to the ground on their bellies. The second round does the trick to keep their heads down and third convinces them there is a formidable enemy to their front.

Sgt. Hoeppner signals for his men to slip back into the woods and disappear like thieves in the night.

Colonel Taylor along with the 10th and 74th arrives back behind the Union line of General Reynolds division.

Taylor gets his men settled down with some food after a long spell that seemed like days since they last ate. He then arranges for ammunition to be supplied, and finally lets his men get some needed rest after fending off the constant onslaughts from the rebels.

Right now a sip of water is a blessing and the peaceful silence is God sent following the haunting sounds of screaming men.

General Reynolds stops by to talk with Colonel Taylor. "Colonel, sit down please I saw you arrive, and I just need to ask you a few questions.

Colonel could you estimate the strength of the Rebel force you faced today, where they could be now and where you think they might be headed next?"

"General Sir, the Rebs are everywhere out there and I'm afraid we've only seen the least of them. They will be behind us soon if we don't get some help. The way I see it they've managed to separate us from the XX Corp and our chances of winning this contest may be on melting ice.

Reynolds absorbs everything he is saying and finds it very disturbing listening to the dour predictions from Colonel Taylor, even though he figured as much. The Rebels have out flanked them and penetrated their lines in many places and are thus achieving success behind the lines.

"A new fight will start here and now" Reynolds says. I need time, time to get back and join General Johnson's division. Our two divisions together are better than one against so many of these rebellious bastards.

Reynolds decides on a bazaar plan of action that might slow the Rebels down enough to buy him the time he needs. To do that though he'll have to ask men to go out and in all probability get killed or captured.

A difficult decision for sure, but he was hired to kill the enemy, not hired to keep his men out of harms way.

Reynolds pays a visit to the regimental commander of the 105th Ohio, Major George Perkin to discuss the plan he has in mind for him.

"Major we are in desperate peril of losing this Army. What I am going to ask you is nothing short of desperation. I need time to swing this division around and move north to join General Johnson. To buy us that time I'm asking you to take your regiment and push into the enemy's lines to create as much havoc amongst them as you can."

The Major after listening to Reynolds suicidal plan takes a long deep breath and then says, "are you asking me to do this or ordering me to do this?"

Reynolds sort of grins at the humorous response, realizing he has selected the right man for the job by his question says, "How does ordering sound to you Major?"

"Well, General Reynolds it certainly eliminates my choices doesn't it. When do I begin this fateful adventure?" "Right away Major Perkins" Reynolds replies.

Perkins salutes Reynolds sharply and says with a rather reserved voice "what the hell General this is as good time as any to finish my business here." With that said Major Perkins hollers to his second in command "Captain form up the regiment, Companies abreast and fix bayonets, we've got some killen to do."

Captain Harris stares at Perkins for a second with a quizzical look. He can tell this isn't the time for questions so he turns and calls out for 1st Sgt. Clarkson to pass the word to fall in.

No formal send off and no idea of how far this journey may take them, Major Perkin with Captain Harris by his side leads the 105th Ohio through the Poe Field that is littered with many of the dead from the last two days fighting, and enters the woods marching south. The woods stink with the stench of the dead sprawled about amongst the trees.

Captain Harris breaks the silence and queries Major Perkins "Major is it to much to ask what is our mission?"

"Captain we are decoyed into these woods to attract the enemies attention." Harris then says rather sarcastically "and what are we to do with these attractions?"

"Kill as many as we can for as long as we last Captain. We will take no prisoners and there will be no going back."

It doesn't take long before they come across their first sighting of the enemy. It appears to be a contingent of Rebels meandering about disorganized with no pickets on guard. The Rebs lying a couple hundred yards off of Perkin's right appear to be a gathering of stragglers. Easy prey to begin their foray in the enemy held territory.

"Captain have Company B quietly, I repeat quietly make an oblique move to the right," Perkin orders.

The Company abreast to the far left slowly swings around to the right. Perkin then whispers for the men to kneel on one knee and prepare to fire when ordered.

The poor rabble of Rebs, haven't as yet discovered Perkin's presence. Resting and lounging about after their flight from the hard charging Indiana boys a couple of hours back, Benning's Georgians have had it with suicidal charges they've been called on to make.

But suddenly their peaceful setting is torn asunder when the muskets from Perkin's regiment opens up with a lethal volley of lead, scattering the Rebels like fallen leaves in the wind. Many are dropped instantly, while the rest take off like startled Quail. Perkin signals to cease firing since no fight is left in these Rebels.

Major Perkin takes a squad to inspect the area that is now deserted excepting only the dead and a few badly wounded with no hope for aide.

Perkin returns and orders Captain Harris to form the men up in column of twos to move out quickly.

The regiment marches away winding their way deeper into enemy territory like a long blue snake. At times they pass by exhausted Rebels who no longer have the will to fight, so they leave them alone without incidence.

After marching for an hour Major Perkin has something to get off his chest.

"Captain I am disturbed by what happened back there. I feel like an executioner. Many of those men we killed were defenseless. I noticed many of them weren't even armed. I don't know where they had been or why they were there, but hell that was like shooting children in a schoolyard. That's not war, that's murder."

"Major, they were enemy soldiers not children in a school yard, and to know the why and where you'd have to have a spy in their encampment. No Major that was not murder that is the unpleasantness of war."

"Captain you know our mission. There is no going back the way we came. I've changed my mind now quite frankly. We will not seek out trouble that could get us trapped against some bad odds. I'm going to do my best to get us out of this fix. We will fight if we have to, but only if we have too. We'll not head any further south we will turn to the west and head for the mountains.

CHAPTER 40

Signs of a battle heard off in the distance are further evidence by the white haze rising above the trees and the rumbling sounds of cannon fire.

The thought once again races across Judd's mind, "men are dieing less than a mile away and here he stands on the edge between living and dieing, confused, and looking for an answer, as he awaits his fate to kill or be killed.

Suddenly he no longer wonders what it was that brought him here. It becomes obviously clear. It was the rush for glory a chance to prove his bravery. Not the drummers drumming and the bands playing, although that may have been apart of it. His stupid age was the real reason, just a simple young boy seeking adventure far from the safety of his childhood home. The pictures he visualized in his mind then of facing the dangers, didn't include the bloody messes and the stench of putrefying flesh or of seeing his friend die in his arms. The enemy was suppose to fall dead and disappear, leaving no grotesque traces behind.

The Army is to be supplied with all the food a soldier could want and clothed in clean smart looking uniforms. But he has neither of these things.

It finally dawns on him that he doesn't belong here. He is trapped, a trap set of his own making. He has no interest in killing anyone like Pa Jones professes and he certainly has no interest in dieing God forbid.

Judd watches Lt. Bishop raise his saber above his head. The sun's rays reflects off his blade a blinding light that sears into his eyes.

Like a baby born from the womb Judd is suddenly thrust back to reality and into a new world wrought with chaos and paralyzing fear.

His very inner sole prays to be rescued, even though down deep he knows he must face his own selfish demons or forever hate himself.

Lt. Bishop leads the way with Sergeant Sawyer by his side a few steps in front Judd and Zach Singer, Chuck Hartely, Pa Jones and the rest of the company in the 44th Mississippi doing duty with General Patton Anderson's two thousand man brigade. Leaving the protection of the woods they emerge out of the shade into the sun lit clearing. The men instinctively crouch lower and move a little slower. Their eyes stinging from the bright sun light hurry to refocus so they can see if the Yankees are close by. So far there is no sign of the dark blue uniforms to be seen. Someone hollers "hey Pa maybe them Yanks heard you was a comin to shop their goods, so they done and disappeared." The humor breaks the tension and lightens the load a bit.

The Union forces in the southern portion of dyer field are desperately fighting to survive. They no longer are concerned with the political causes that have brought them to this. The preservation of the Union doesn't mean a dickers damn if you are dead. And for most, the abolishment of slavery isn't even a thought. They are fighting to stay alive, and to protect their pals from the overwhelming Confederate forces pressing hard to destroy each and every one of them.

The further west the Rebs push the battle, the greater the chance they will be able to roll up the Federal line and smash what is left of Rosecran's Army.

The Union threat in the Deep South will be crushed and the Confederate forces down deep in Dixie will be free to join Lee's Army in Virgina.

Confederate General Zachrey Deas has had his hands full since the assault began today, trying to dislodge the stubborn defenses of General Jefferson Davis's division.

Approaching on his left and several hundred yards to the east Deas's support under General Patton Anderson's has yet to meet the enemy.

General Davis's whittled down division is outmatched and faltering fast.

General McCook's Corp is quickly running out of time and divisions to throw in against the swelling ranks of the gray scourge.

General Davis leaves the field out of desperation to find help to save his meager division. His only hope is to locate General Sheridan.

Sheridan realizes the whole Union line is facing catastrophic consequences for not using the whole might of Rosecran's Army in the beginning when Bragg started his attack two days ago.

General Davis in his quest to find Sheridan at first comes upon Colonel Laiboldt leading the first brigade in Sheridan's division.

Laiboldt's brigade is marching along the top of a ridge arrayed in the traditional defensive stack that provides an unquestionable advantage over an aggressor.

"Colonel I need you to order your brigade forward immediately, my division is in peril of being overrun," Davis shouts.

Liablodt takes a second to look over the sweating General and senses his fear. General Davis becomes extremely agitated by Liaboldt's slow reaction towards him and his disregard to quickly act.

"General I am under orders from General Sheridan. I can do a better job here on this high ground and you could too by moving your division up here, as you can see it is a lot more defendable," Liaboldt says.

"Colonel I am not asking you for advice and I do not have the time to argue. I am ordering you to move your men forward without further delay."

General McCook sees Davis and hurries over to get some news on what's happening on the line. Davis seizes this opportunity to report on the desperate situation facing his division and the refusal by Colonel Laiboldt to prompty engage his brigade.

"General McCook sir as you can see I am formed up to defend this higher ground" Liaboldt explains.

Davis interrupts "General McCook I don't care if he has Heaven under his boots, my men can't hang on much longer if we don't bring them some help. They are dieing as we speak sir!"

Now Liablodt gets desperate to plead his case, stating that he would have to have the time to reorganize his brigade to go on the offensive.

Davis then says in despair "there isn't time!"

McCook agrees with Davis and orders Colonel Laiboldt to move to the front in his present formation.

Liaboldt has no choice now but to obey the Corp Commander even though he strongly feels the order is a death knell for his brigade.

Liaboldt regretfully orders his leading regiment the 73rd Illinois to begin the trek down the ridge followed by his other three regiments stacked one behind the other. The breadth of each regiment measures less than a hundred yards across from flank to flank.

The somber attitude of the 73rd is obvious and betrays the lack of commitment for the task at hand.

Colonel Jacquess leading the regiment understands that the seasoned men are aware they shouldn't be formed up in a parade formation and marched off like this into battle.

Jacquess also understands to have a decent chance these men will need to be fired up and positive about their chances. He wonders aloud "what's he to do?" He has been ordered to rush in and do the impossible.

Colonel Jacquess a Methodist minister before the war knows the power of prayer and also the power of a song.

Jacquess decides if they must go, by God they'll go out with a song on their lips. He then breaks the silence and begins singing the song "Battle Cry for Freedom."

The men at first look to him as if he has lost his senses.

The Colonel rides back and pulls up along side the regiment and hollers, "come on men lets scare the devil out of them Rebs. Sing!"

He begins again singing, "Yes we'll rally around the flag boys, we'll rally around once again, shouting the Battle Cry of Freedom…"

Slowly the men join in and the volume picks up to a rowdy rendition of "we'll rally around the flag boys" as they continue marching down the ridge and onto the Dyer Field, proudly marching into the thick of battle disappearing in the smoke singing their song.

The mood is contagious, behind them the 15th Missouri is singing "Bonnie Blue Flag…we're fighting for our Union, we're fighting for our trust…Hurrah for the good old flag that bears the stripes and stars…

Liaboldt's adversary General Zachery Deas with his Alabama brigade has his regiments stretched out side by side that measures at least six times wider than Liaboldt's stacked regiments. To make matters worse for Liaboldt's difficult task, General Patton Anderson's Mississippi brigade is on the way to add support to Deas's left flank.

General Sheridan is livid upon learning of the order that sent Liaboldt's brigade into a fight that has little chance for success. He doesn't waste any strong lanuage criticizing General McCook for his lack of judgment.

Sheridan promptly deploys his second brigade under General William Lytle to race to the side of Liaboldt. This time the regiments are arrayed properly side by side

Time is crucial but time runs out quickly for Liaboldt.

General Deas larger force easily overlaps Liaboldt's both flanks and dispatches him soon after finishing off General Jefferson Davis's division.

Deas's tired brigade, to exhausted, to chase after the routed Yanks, sets up an impregnable wall of men who pour out a continuous volley of lead into Lytle's arriving regiments.

Sheridan doesn't spare a man as he sends in his final brigade, commanded by Colonel Nathan Walworth, to fight on the right side of Lytle's flank.

Deas's long line of Alabamians is bolstered by the arrival of General Anderson's Mississippians on his left.

The battle escalates furiously along Sheridan's three quarter mile front.

CHAPTER 41

Judd Archer in the company of the 44th Mississippi has as yet to ever see a Yankee dead or otherwise.

His platoon has just left the clearing and is slowly making their way through the woods.

The sound of musketry and smoke of battle hangs thick as they get closer to the front. Judd experiences something he has only imagined up till now.

Judd keeps an eye on Pa Jones, and tries to copy the way Pa is crouched over weaving his way around the trees step for step.

The regimental colors are furled around the flagstaff to keep the precious flag from damage by the foliage.

A strange pffing sound zips past Judd's ear. A small branch falls to the ground just behind him. Judd ducks down and notices Pa crouch down even lower.

Lt. Bishop's saber he is holding over his shoulder is suddenly blasted out of his hand, sending the blade flailing through the air.

Judd is sure that incident must have hurt Bishop's hand, but Bishop says nothing and maintains his composure, even though he's damn lucky he didn't lose his hand.

Bishop pauses and kneels down to get a better look at the front under the hanging smoke. The smoke is extremely dense and hard to see through. The smokes Sulfurous content makes it most difficult to breathe as well.

Judd has finally reached a battlefield. His feelings are teetering between excitement and panic. His heart is pounding so hard he fears someone must hear it.

A soldier off to the left is sent reeling backwards hardly making a sound. Judd has no idea who the man was since he was so far away. Zach Singer and Chick Hartley are over that way Judd hopes it wasn't either of them. He dismisses the thought from his mind when he becomes more concerned with what Pa Jones is doing. He quickly glances over to his right to see Pa squatting down waiting with the rest to begin moving forward again.

Lt. Bishop with his pistol in his hand signals the men forward.

Now getting ever closer to the front the sounds of battle are becoming louder and more distinct. Wild shots are heard striking the trees overhead. A scream is heard further back somewhere in the woods.

Judd gets a little more shaken as one thought after another, races through his mind. Will he be killed without ever seeing the enemy or ever firing a shot?

Bishop shouts "double quick to the front" as he picks up the pace.

Shouts and cries are heard in every direction. Judd keeps pace with the others keeping an eye on Pa. Ear shattering racket from the thousands of muskets and artillery shells exploding, and adding the hundreds men shouting with many screaming from pain.

Pa stops running and falls to one knee and fires his musket, loads and fires again. Judd tries to see what he is shooting at but he quickly jumps behind a tree to take shelter from the many bullets zipping past.

Judd slowly takes a chance and peers around the tree. There not a hundred yards away Judd sees the enemy for the first time.

Yankees, marching damn near shoulder to shoulder kneel down behind whatever cover they can find to fire and reload. Judd instinctively ducks back behind the tree. He notices the others are actively engaged, and he is the only one not firing at the enemy. They've got to be plum stupid to expose themselves that way he thinks.

A corporal, Judd has never seen before slides up beside his tree and kneels to take a shot. The stranger notices Judd doing nothing and says "you something special boy? If you ain't gonna shoot you can damn well load my musket while I use yours."

Judd stares at the stranger, feeling a sense of shame wash over his body with a shiver. He glances over at Pa still kneeling a short distance away firing as fast as he can load.

The corporal grabs Judd's musket and shoves his into Judd's stomach saying "load it damn it!"

Judd's hands trembling as he pushes the ball down the barrel and hands it to the stranger. The corporal then takes aim and squeezes the trigger; nothing happens. He turns the rifle upside down and the ball falls out on the ground. The exasperated corporal says "boy you aint worth your momma's labor. Don't you know you gotta put some powder in there before the damn ball?"

Those are the last words out of the stranger's mouth. His head is ripped from his body in a flash by a cannon ball screaming past. Judd trembling in shock looks down on the body and does everything he can to keep from regurgitating. He gathers himself together and timidly reaches out from the protection of the tree and yanks the musket out of the frozen grip of the dead corporal's hand. Jerking the musket back to his belly he begins loading the powder charge and ramming the ball down the barrel. He glances over at Pa kneeling like a ramrod in his tattered worn pants, busy doing what a real soldier does.

Judd takes a deep breath and steps out from behind the tree and without taking aim fires, and then quickly jumps back behind his cover. Repeating the process over and over, he is in a world void of anyone else, a world where he is all alone, one of reaction not of reason. He also begins to feel a bit proud, having found the courage to step out from the tree. He's becoming battle hardened he concludes. Then the truth hits him square the gut. He is shooting for no good purpose at all, just shooting at nothing.

Judd reloads and steps away from the tree, but this time he takes his time standing out from the protection of his tree. Standing out in the open, exposed too enemy fire in the dense smoke circulating around his body, he strains to see the enemy. The Yankees are moving back, but they are still firing but a short distance away.

Bishop's voice can be heard above the clamor of battle hollering "let's go get them boys, they're running off" he shouts.

Judd notices Pa still kneeling to take another shot before he rises to his feet.

Judd takes another look back at the enemy and raises the butt of his musket to his shoulder and sets his eye behind the sight. He sets the sight on a ghostly figure clothed in dark blue. Taking aim Judd squeezes down on the trigger. He squints through the smoke over the musket to see if his aim has been true. The figure in the smoke sort of staggers back and drops his rifle before falling out of sight in the swirling smoke.

Judd feels something he doesn't quite understand. He should feel all powerful, rejoicing for he has become a legitimate veteran now. He has just made his first kill. He has slain the enemy in battle, isn't that what it is all about. But he feels none of these things, he feels sick and somewhat dirty, guilty, a loss of innocence.

It then dawns on him that there had to be others shooting at the same target. How can one be sure they made the shot that counted? No it couldn't have been him, he's not that good of a soldier. He suddenly feels cleansed and not guilty.

Judd shoulders his musket and starts moving out with the rest of the platoon, not needing now to watch Pa Jones anymore, he's his own man now.

Less than ten yards to Judd's front a blast sends a shower of dirt, smoke, and white hot shrapnel through the air in all directions. The concussion from the shell tears at everything near by. The suddenness by which this destructive blast came, mixed with its choking smoke, conversely just as suddenly the smoke slowly begins to evaporated with the breeze.

CHAPTER 42

No man should ever have to face this carnage that is inflicted on both of the adversaries struggling for supremacy along the Dyer, Brock, and Viniard Fields.

The heavy caliber hollow projectiles make a mess of whatever it strikes. Both the Blue and the Gray suffer the consequences. The Blue however is suffering the most along the Chickamauga.

General Lytle's undermanned brigade, survivors of yesterday's action, is caving to the pressure brought on by General Deas and Anderson's relentless attacks.

Colonel Walworth is doing all he can on Lytle's right to stave off the enemy, but he too is barely hanging on.

General Lytle is trying to organize an orderly pull back. His thinning ranks are no match against Deas and Andersons over whelming forces any longer.

Lytle doesn't get a chance to inform Colonel Walworth of his intentions because shortly after he begins to orchestrate his retreat he is shot from his horse by a bullet that blows his face away. Sadly he doesn't live long enough to learn the fate of his effort.

General Longstreet's astonishing battle plan is working superbly throughout the Confederate's left wing for the most part. Of course to say "for the most part" is ambiguous because it leaves one skeptical of the total successes.

The rout of Lytle's right leaves Walworth's left flank defenseless in the face of the invading Rebels swarming over the left side of his line, inflicting irreparable damage to the other two regiments fighting along side.

The survivors scramble and claw their way across the ground to get away from this impossible situation before they too join their comrades spilling their all over the ground.

The erosion in the ranks begins with a few, then mushrooms, as more and more take flight running from the ghastly carnage.

The whole brigade is feeling the effects of this spreading virus that affects the whole chain of command.

On the far left of Longstreet's Corp, an Alabama brigade led by General Arthur Manigualt struggles to overpower three of Walworth's regiments defiantly holding the right of his position.

Some of Manigualt's trouble stems from becoming separated from Anderson's left, caused by the dense smoke shrouding the few miles of the contested front.

At one point however Manigualt had successfully turned Walworth's right flank. That is until the untimely arrival of Colonel John Wilder's "Lightning brigade" with his mounted infantry equipped with their .56 cal. Spencer rifles.

Colonel John Wilder's impromptu appearance along side the flank of Walworth's right is like daylight to a nightmare.

The young thirty two year old Colonel has just the right dose of medicine to calm the feverish state of what's left of Walworth's brigade.

Wilder is gifted with wisdom far beyond his years of experience. It was his idea to equip his men with the newly developed Spencer rifle, and it was his idea that developed the mounted infantry he commands.

Wilder is innovative, smart, and has a whole gut full of courage.

Now Wilder's inexplicable timing catches the Alabamans in a cross-fire that cuts them down like a scythe.

Manigualt's, his short time successes cave in like a mirror image of Lytle's rout. His men scramble east back toward the safety of Longstreet's reserve divisions.

Wilder's brigade pursues Manigualt's force laying down a withering fire that fells many before they can reach safety. Wilder though is more interested to find out something about the enemies strength than finishing off a beaten brigade.

As he nears the LaFayette road he calls off the pursuit when he gets an eyeful of Longstreet's countless reserves positioned throughout the woods.

He quickly summons his regimental commanders and orders them to form up their regiments. While they are forming up he sends Sergeant Braman on a mission to find out what is left of Sheridan's command, and to inform Sheridan about the Confederates reserve strength.

Wilder hastens over to confer with his leading regimental commander Colonel Atkins. "Colonel I believe we may be the only ones left on this end of the line."

"If that's true Colonel Wilder, we'll have hell to pay the devil.

Wilder pauses for minute and then says "Colonel have the brigade form up the regiments parallel east and west, North to south. Double up the North side."

Atkin very familiar with Wilder's innovative mind doesn't question his intentions and goes about as he is ordered.

On a larger scale this formation is really nothing new. The Roman legions used this formation effectively to protect the Legions from every direction the enemy might use to make an assault. Wilder's intention here is to use the Spencer as both the shield and the sword. However the Roman Legions didn't have to deal with explosive artillery.

Sergeant Braman returns as Wilder is moving the formation through the Viniard Field.

"Colonel Wilder sir" Braman says somewhat out of breath from his hard ride, "I've got rather bad news."

"Sergeant I hardly expected good," Wilder responds.

"Well Colonel General Sheridan has gathered up what's left of his division, and is headed west toward the mountain ridge. What his reasons are I can't say, I didn't take the time, I thought it best I get back here."

"Very good Sergeant, but could you see where the Rebs are headed?"

"Hard to say, but it looks as if they could be turning toward the north, you know there is still a lot of racket up that way. Can't blame them much for getting the hell out of here, this grave yard is going to stink to high heaven pretty damn quick," Braman says as he spits out tobacco juice.

Wilder quietly ponders his options for a minute as he rides along with Atkin. Atkin breaks the silence "we could make better time in a column of twos."

"I agree completely, if I knew which way I was going. I was considering crashing through the Confederate lines to join Thomas. Right straight through them"

Colonel Atkin leans over to pet his horse's neck as he passes by the body of a dead horse, thinking to himself how he doesn't have the same sadness for the dead soldiers.

He seems to have grown impervious to the killing. He says to Wilder "I think I'll send out a squad, see if can't pick up some stray horses."

"Good thinking Colonel, what I've got in mind I think we'll need them, and probably a lot more to boot."

Wilder looks over at Atkin, "you've got a stake in this, any opinions?" he says.

"I'm skeptical," Atkin answers.

Sergeant Braman rides up beside Wilder and points to a single rider coming towards them at a fast gait.

"Sergeant go and take a look see,"

Braman pulls his pistol, sinks his spurs into the horse and bolts away. He fires a shot in the air and then another. The stranger waves his hands frantically as Braman races toward him.

Braman pulls up close to the stranger in civilian clothes and shouts "hold it right there."

The stranger continues waving and yelling, "I'm Charles Dana, assistant Secretary of war. I've come for your help."

Braman trots his horse up beside the man his pistol aimed toward his head.

The unnerved man pleads, "I'm Charles Dana assistant Secretary of war to Edwin Stanton. I need help from your commander Sergeant. Please understand I need to hurry."

Braman searches Dana's excited eyes for a sign of legitimacy. "Mr. Dana follow me, I'll take you to Colonel Wilder."

The two hastily ride up to the waiting Colonels, and before Braman can say a word Dana blurts out who he is and rants "Colonel it's imperative you escort me as quickly as possible to Chattanooga, I've got to telegraph the Secretary."

"Mr. Dana if you haven't noticed I'm busy fighting a war here."

"Colonel what war, they have destroyed our Army here. All is lost Sir and I can't take a chance of becoming a prisoner."

"Mr. Dana you hear that racket to the north, this Army isn't finished obviously, and I am going to the sound of that battle. I can only spare an escort, but that is all I can do."

"Colonel that racket you hear is the Rebels finishing off General Thomas.

Wilder gives the pathetic Dana a disdainful look hating him for his cowardly behavior. He turns his face away preferring not to look at him. Wilder says "suppose you tell me where General Rosecran is and we will put this problem in his lap."

Dana's becomes desperate and more demanding. "Rosecran hell I haven't seen Rosecran since morning. For all I know he may be dead or captured. Colonel I am ordering you to escort me to Chattanooga without any further argument or delay.

"You just sit still a moment Mr. Dana," Wilder shouts back. "You are ordering me? I'm not convinced I fall into your realm of authority. This is a fighting unit with the responsibility to fight the enemy which does not include the responsibility to escort civilians off a battlefield."

Atkin interrupts, "Colonel Wilder I'm not so sure. He may very well have that authority as assistant Secretary of War.

Wilder stares angrily at Atkin for a moment surprised by his comment.

The noise from the battle toward the north nags at Wilder's moral sense of duty as he considers his choices.

Once again Dana speaks out, "Colonel Wilder I implore you Sir to listen to reason. The Government needs to learn what has happened here. They will need to make the necessary plans to counter this terrible debacle."

Wilder peers back at Atkin and then his waiting brigade. Wilder then issues his orders "Colonel Atkin reform the brigade, column of fours, scouts out forward and to the right. Pick up all stray mounts along the way. We will proceed west through Missionary Ridge and escort this gentleman to Tennessee. Then we will proceed and join General Thomas on the battlefield. Mr. Dana shall ride along with your command Colonel Atkin."

Colonel Atkin offers a stiff salute, and wheels his horse around with Dana and begins to ride away when Wilder calls to him. Atkin hesitates then rides back to see what his commander wants now.

Wilder apologetically says to Atkin, "Colonel I appreciate your council, if you are right you've saved me a heap of trouble, and if you are wrong you probably saved my life. Either way, please keep that gentleman out of my sight." Atkin smiles and turns his horse back around and rides off to his command.

Wilder and his "lightning Brigade", ride away from the ground strewn with the bodies of his enemy that he so skillfully put there. Now he needs to skillfully get his command through the passes and hurry to Chattanooga so he can once again get back into the fight.

All the while Sheridan is struggling to hang on along the western portion of the Viniard and Brock fields, the northern part of the struggle is taking place on the edge of woods bordering the west side of the Dyer Field.

An auspicious Union commander Major Mendenhall has been ordered to establish an extensive line of artillery along a plateau atop a ridge facing south.

Confederate General Bushrond Johnson's division is assigned to take this ground. Johnson's three brigades led by General McNair, Colonel Sugg and Colonel Fulton are spread out nearly half a mile across the area and are determined to carry the ridge.

Two small Union regiments stand between the massive Rebel front and Mendenhall's guns. These two regiments don't need a lot of persuasion to come to a conclusion they need to get out of the way and run back to the guns when they get an eye full of the enemy force headed their way.

Major Mendenhall waits for the Rebels to close where his cannons can be the most effective. He then orders his artillery to open up with everything they have. Double canister, three inch and six inch shot slows McNair's brigade considerably. However Fulton's brigade is spared the brunt of the Union barrage, since he is clamoring up off Mendenhall's right flank.

Mendenhall isn't totally blinded by the smoke he can see well enough to realize his line of artillery is close to becoming flanked on the right and has no chance of survival.

Many of the horses harnessed to the caissons are either dead from the Confederate fire or crazed by the horrendous noise and no longer are useful to remove the cannon. He orders the gun crews to cut the surviving horses loose and then too save themselves.

The raucous horde of Rebels arriving atop the plateau shout and cheer with merriment over the taking of the prized cannons still sizzling from the explosive gunpowder and left abandoned by the retreating Yankees.

Hardily celebrating the capture of the guns they forget the price they paid with the many lives of their brethren lying scattered across the slope torn to pieces.

General McNair feels the pain though for his action, he is carried from the field severely wounded. His revelry will have to wait if he survives.

The tired and spent conquerors halt their onslaught and hold up on the plateau to rest and rearm, gratis the Yankees ammunition wagons that also fell into their hands.

Bushrod Johnson has no intention of letting up the pressure. A wise man doesn't step on the head of a poisonous snake and step off without killing the snake first.

The Federals have wisely pushed back and are consolidating what they can upon a hilly ground known as Horseshoe Ridge.

Johnson orders General Jerome Robertson to lead his Texas brigade north through the Dyer Field. Robertson's left flank will have protection from three regiments of Alabamians and his rear will have the support from a brigade of South Carolinians.

Robertson's Texans are not long off the train from Virginia and have been newly supplied with uniforms purchased from an English company. The only other brigade sporting these new uniforms is General Joseph Kershaw's South Carolinians also off the train from Virginia.

Nearly all the troops in Bragg's army are clothed in a mishmash of homespun fabrics and colors of grays and tans commonly known as butternut that for the most part have been worn to tatters.

The trouble for the newly outfitted brigades is their coats are dyed a dark bluish gray and their trousers are of a light blue color. In smoky conditions they could easily be mistaken for the Yankee issue.

Colonel Perry with his three Alabama regiments slowly works north through an edge of woods taking care to keep a watchful eye for Federal ambushers. Perry is aware Robertson is suppose to be moving along on his right but he can't comfortably confirm who or what is making the disturbing noise he can hear, so to be safe Perry sends a scouting patrol out to determine the source.

The Sergeant in command of the patrol, quietly peers through the foliage and discovers laid out before him a great number of troops in dark uniforms steadily moving north toting regimental flags he is unfamiliar with. He silently backs away and leaves the area quickly to report his findings.

Colonel Perry listens to the Sergeants report and replies "Well done Sergeant, I received a communiqué that confirms we are shadowing a brigade of Texans moving across the cultivated field on our right.

"Yes sir the Sergeant replies, but these Texans sure are outfitted in mighty fine uniforms, nothing like I've seen around here excepten maybe them Yanks. You could damn sure mistake them when powder smoke gets bad. Perry picks up on the Sergeants doubtful remark but lets it rest for the time being.

CHAPTER 42

A hodgepodge of Union brigades, regiments, and smaller units with plenty of fight left collect upon and around the ground on Snodgrass Hill.

Dug in and maintaining a watch in the timber is the 78th PA. from General Negley's division.

Privates John Davis, James Farr, and Henry Long lay in their dugout loaded and ready for the Rebs. Thus far they've been spared the rigors of the fight having been assigned reserve duty for the past two days. Never the less they have experienced the acrid smoke from the battles leaving them with itchy eyes and a nagging cough. They've seen the soldiers crawling back shaken or wounded from their dances with the enemy.

"Damn Davis how in the hell can you eat that mess that taste so much like it was cooked in sulfur grease?" Farr ask.

The two soldiers close, as brothers need each other as they need food or water. Private Long also a part of this brotherhood is more reserved and less opinionated. The three have been campaigning together through the Tennessee campaigns before marching into Georgia.

"You know Farr you oughta give some of this grub a chance, it could be your last bite before the Devil comes and snatches your poor lousy soul off." Davis quips.

"Aint no Devil coming for us anytime soon I'll bet ya. I aint so sure we'll ever dirty a cartridge in this here fight," Long adds.

Several hundred yards to their front they can clearly hear the bone chilling throaty sounds of men yelling and the roar of musketry.

Sergeant Drake shuffles up behind their dugout and growls "Second squad Company B fall out and muster for latrine detail, double quick."

Private Davis turns and looks at the Sergeant with an expression of disbelief.

Enemy action taking place not that far off, and here they are ordered to leave and dig a latrine. Davis slams his fist down in the dirt and says "Damn Sergeant we had that lousy detail two days ago." The others chime in their complaints as well.

Sergeant Drake isn't moved and has no patience for their opinions about anything they want to say. He earned his stripes in the regular Army before the war the hard way, enduring long and arduous abhorring chores.

Drake once again growls "Second squad Company B fall out for muster double quick.

The men slowly but surely fall in and line up to face the Sergeant and count off. After the muster is completed, Drake orders the men to stack arms and take shovels and picks lying on the ground nearby and follow him. They march off into the woods for a half hour or so before the Sergeant Drake halts them on a piece of level ground. He picks up four rocks and lays out a defining pattern for them to use to shape the trench.

One of the privates often referred to as Teacher because of his scholarly background ask, "Sergeant how did we come by this illustrious privilege to be appointed this task?"

Sergeant Drake caught a bit off guard responds curtly, "Well soldier since you need to know how you qualified for this important duty I'll try to keep it simple so you can understand, you being an educated man and all. Would it have been better to select men who have fought without letup for the last two days to sling a shovel for their reward, or do you think food and rest would suit their portion?

Now you and your brave comrades start digging and dig it deep and straight."

CHAPTER 43

The 21st Ohio materializes out of the woods like some apparitions swelling out from the mist only the mist is sulfurous smoke. They let loose a barrage in the side of Roberson's Texans on the left.

Within a matter of seconds they fire four more volleys from their Colt five shot rifles, instantly sending many of the hapless Texans to the hereafter. As quickly as the 21st materialized they just as quickly evaporate back amongst the trees.

The ambush disrupts the cohesion among the Texans ranks that steals away a portion of their determination.

Robertson responds by calling a halt to his brigades advance so his left can recover from this unexpected slaughter and form back up.

General Wood watching through his field glass remarks, "That was amazing, whoever was leading that outfit on that ambush deserves more gold on his shoulders. He may not know it but he's given us the opportunity to pounce on those bastards before they are aware they're dead. Have Colonel Harker's brigade engage them immediately with all the bravado he can muster."

Colonel Harker upon receiving the word orders his brigade forward under orders to implement Rolling Thunder. The advance technique rarely seen that offers minimum exposure to enemy fire but on the other hand offers a constant rate of fire as the men keep moving toward the enemy. The front rank fires a volley then goes to ground to reload while the rear rank steps forward and fires. Four ranks participate in this exercise that takes very little time.

The Texans at best can only fire three rounds a minute, no match against what they are receiving, with the Yankee lead in the air with every breath.

The Texans fall in appalling numbers that creates a panic throughout the survivors.

General John B. Hood having just arrived from Virginia after recovering from a severe wound he received at Gettysburg in July, can't believe his eyes when he witnesses his old command retreating in such disorder. Although still disabled with a paralyzed arm he jumps aboard his horse and races off to spur his old command to regain their composure.

The General rides into the crush shouting insults and encouragements to try and stem the tide of his hysterical brethren. He himself exposed to the dangers from the rain of bullets that are flying every which of way, is finally blasted out of his saddle when a ball penetrates through his upper thigh.

Hood is bleeding profusely from the wound and is carried out of the confusion and from the field by his aides. He demands to be taken first to General Kershaw before he is taken to a medical tent. Once in front of General Kershaw a few minutes later Hood fights to stay conscious and says to Kershaw "General ride with your command and cleanse the field of those invaders. Have your South Carolinians avenge the honor of my Texans Sir." He then closes his eyes and passes out.

Within hearing distance of the struggle taking place between Harker and the Texans General Negley commanding the Union's Second Division isn't at all clear on what is going to his front. Negley unable to sit a horse due to a severe case of dysentery he's been down with and seems to be getting worse is for the most part confined to a bed rigged in a ambulance wagon. Fortunately Negley hasn't had to lead his division in combat since his command has been relegated to reserve duty since Friday.

Negley a brave conscientious officer is not himself, weakened with fever and the harsh effects from his intestinal disorder, who at times now suffers with delirium.

Negley mistakes Harker's triumph over Robertson's Texans for a Confederate breakthrough, mistaking the Union regimental flags for the Confederates.

General Negley dressed in just his trousers and boots struggling to make sense of what is going on, has a one sided conversation with one of his brigade commanders Colonel Sirwell. Negley, convinced all is lost if he hesitates any longer, orders the division to pull out and make way for Rossville.

Colonel Sirwell sensitive to Negley's physical condition, for he knows the debilitating effects from the disease can bring a good man to his knees. But just the same he bluntly disagrees with the General to his face and tells him that to pull out now could have a disastrous effect on the defenses along the ridge. He argues "General you must meet with General Thomas first before we make a move of this nature."

Negley's face reddens with rage over Sirwell's suggestion. "Colonel you listen to me, I'm still in command here, now you get this division on the road. I am not going to lay here and let my division get annihilated. The damn clock is ticking Sir," Negley chokes out. "Now get on with my order."

Colonel Sirwell convinced the General is dead wrong continues to argue "Sir I repeat, General Thomas needs to be informed."

Negley scoffs at Sirwell "Thomas, Thomas, well hell Colonel I haven't seen hide nor hair of Thomas since who knows when. Maybe he's left without informing me. Maybe he isn't even still alive. Hell this entire campaign is about to fall to pieces. Colonel you get this division on the road to Rossville, and I don't want to hear any more about this, you hear me Sir?"

Negley his face flushed, staggers to climb back into wagon, as Sirwell looks on in disgust.

CHAPTER 44

Colonel Harker's success over Robertson's Texans isn't the battle but only another step on the road to glory or dispair.

Colonel Harker's brigade has been under the gun since yesterday and is sorely weakened for not receiving needed replacements. He now learns that the 21st Ohio protecting his right flank is ordered to pull back and rejoin General Brannan's brigade.

Harker is no fool cause with his right left unprotected he knows he must prepare to give back the ground his men fought so hard to take.

Confederate General Joseph Kershaw is no fool either, he is well aware he has the numerical advantage by what he can see from his vantage point. He quickly devises a tactical plan to catch the Yanks in a deadly crossfire on all three of their fronts.

He plans to send the 2nd South Carolina regiment off on a wide circle to the west to take a position off the Union right flank. On the other side of the Union line he will send the 8th South Carolina around on a wide arc to the east to flank the Union left. His remaining five regiments will attack up the middle, which should attract the Yanks complete attention, allowing the flanking forces to garner his desired surprise.

Tactical warfare is a game of opportunity and a game of chance, with Time always the common denominator.

Now is the Time to take a chance on the opportunity afforded him.

General Kershaw's hole card is General Humphreys Mississippi brigade trailing not far off on his right wing.

The five leading regiments are in no hurry so to allow enough time for the flanking regiments to reach their appointed positions, steadily march toward the Yankee line that has as yet to pull back.

Stranger than strange, Kershaw is receiving absolutely no resistance from the Union front. Kershaw of course has no idea that their dark uniforms are causing the Yanks to second guess his identity.

General Thomas confers with General Wood and Colonel Harker and suggested the approaching troops could be that of General Sheridan's division on his way to join them.

Thomas doesn't order Harker but suggest he have his regiments wave their regimental flags back and forth rapidly. If it is friends approaching they'll return the signal, and if not he will have them in his sights.

The idea certainly makes common sense, but not to the South Carolinians. They take the signal as an insult, thinking the Yanks are taunting them.

These Rebels commonly known as the "Gamecocks" from South Carolina wave their colors back in defiance.

The ruse backfires on the Yanks, but works beautifully for the Gamecocks. At least until they get close enough for the Federals to read the words South Carolina across one of the regimental flags. The white of their eyes are as clear as a Firefly and their dark coats aren't navy but dark gray.

All hell breaks loose and at a very close range.

The Yanks outnumbered still make a hell'va stand fighting savagely with all the fiber of their being, until the surprise crossfire is unleashed on their flank by the 2nd South Carolinian regiment.

One unit after another on Harker's right begins to fall. The very thing that worried him in the first place is now happening.

Harker gives the order to retreat and take refuge from the storm of bullets caused by the deadly crossfire. Harker's Yanks work their way back to Snodgrass field and joins General Beatty's brigade.

The 2nd South Carolinians doesn't hesitate to charge out of the woods in pursuit. That is when the 2nd runs smack up against the 21st Ohio dug in atop a steep ridge on the west side of Brannan's Union line now positioned across Horseshoe Ridge's high ground.

The 21st Ohio's five shot revolving rifles lay down a withering wall of lead into the Gamecocks attempting to climb the steep slope. The Gamecocks can't withstand this kind of firepower and are forced to retreat back down the slope to take cover and wait for the rest of the brigade to arrive.

General Bushrod Johnson's division is faced with the problem of trying to dislodge a large force that holds the high ground. A ground configured by steep draws and three plateaus protruding out naturally providing the defenders a lethal crossfire position.

General Kershaw arrives with his brigade and immediately orders an assault up the Horseshoe Ridge supported on the right by General Humphreys Mississippi brigade.

Twice they try to claw their way up the steep slope and both times they are shot to pieces for their effort.

General Humphreys a cautious natured man realizes the futility of attacking up the steep ridge against a dug in and determined foe. It is a fools chance to take without an overwhelming force around him, and twice now they have tried at a waste of many a good man.

No, Humphreys decides to pull back to reconsider his options and find a better way, when he is surprised to see General Longstreet and his staff ride up.

Humphreys cordially greets the famed General and reluctantly informs him of his decision to pull back and why.

Longstreet listens to Humphreys dilemma and is sympathetic since he has garnered from his recent experiences and concluded that a frontal assault against a formidable position piecemeal is a recipe for disaster.

New technology already gained since the war started has made the time honored tactic obsolete.

The bold fearless method of attacking shoulder to shoulder against a barricaded enemy without effective artillery has proved fruitless, a.k.a. Gettysburg.

In this heavily wooded terrain a long distant artillery bombardment is not an option.

Longstreet tells him flanking the enemy with a coordinated frontal assault is the only way to get the job done. A lot of men, a lot of missiles in the air at the same time will make the Yanks position untenable.

Longstreet then adds, "You sit tight and wait till I get a couple of brigades from General Hindman's division to bring help over on the left so we can flank the son of a bitches then you get after their throat. We'll take that ridge and avenge what has happened here."

Colonels Fulton and Sugg lead their brigades of Tennessee troops on a climb up the northwestern slope of the Horseshoe Ridge.

General Kershaw's troops not completely recovered from their previous attempt to take the heights from the stubborn Yanks, struggle once again along side Hindman's Mississippians to gain the foothold on top of Horseshoe Ridge.

Pa Jones and Zach Singer lay hugging the ground together, trying to figure out a way to escape the rain of bullets that are pelting the ground all around them.

"They done got us this time." Zach hollers. "Kinda looks that way now don't it, but ifin they hadn't kilt us by now on that last climb, it could be we got someone high up a looking after us." Pa yells back. "Don't know nuthin about that, but I do know I aint never been this scaret like this before." Zach admits.

"Well Zach old boy there aint no time betterin this to come to know the Lord, cause you damn sure gonna need em soon enough."

In a somber tone, Pa adds, "I done hope Chick Hartely sure enough knowed the Lord." Zach turns and peers at Pa and says, "Chick Hartlely?" Pa nods and says, " saws him take a slew of hits. He'd be layin up there bloodless by now. That be why we done and need to get our selves free from here, so's we can get home and tell the folks how we done and whipped the Yank for killin guys like old Chick. You hear me boy. On three we gonna jump and run like skitterin Hares." "Three! Lets get goin."

CHAPTER 45

A young man trips and staggers over the refuse of war. His hair is singed off and his face puffy and ashen.

He shuffles along through the haze in a daze; his mind struggles to comprehend what he sees around him. He falls as he tries to avoid contact with what appears to be the wreckage of human remains. The sounds of battle some distance away is muffled by the loud ringing in his ears.

Weak and worn out he flops down on a fallen tree trunk to catch his breath. He notices his bare bleeding legs through what is left of his shredded trousers.

Grimacing in pain he also notices his arms and hands are bleeding from small punctures that look to be as bad as his legs.

Thirst overcomes the discomfort he feels and takes over his every thought except the memory of a sudden bright hot flash that enveloped him. The haunting memory fades though with the pressing want for water, cool wet water. He had a canteen with him before, but doesn't have one now and can't figure what happened to it.

The strong drive to gulp down rivers of water has only begun to corrupt his moral fabric, for not far from where he sits his eyes catch sight of a body curled up on the ground. He stares at the body with a sort of weird fascination.

The corpse looks to be that of a young man as far as he can tell from where he sits. It is clothed in the uniform of a Yankee, with the dark blue coat and light blue trousers. A white strap is slung over the neck and shoulder with a canteen on the end lying on the ground.

The realization of this canteen lying there for the taking flushes all other cares from his mind.

He leaps off the tree trunk with all the energy left in his body and scrambles across the ground on his hands and knees like a madman to reach the precious container.

He reaches out to grab for the canteen when he notices the contorted expression frozen on the face of the young soldier. He pauses for a time staring into the eyes, but his thirst is too strong. He frantically pulls at the strap and yanks it over the soldier's head and off the body.

He grasps the canteen and rips at the lid pulling it off and with both hands plunges the neck of the container in his mouth gulping down the water as fast as it will pour, spilling some of it and choking on some of it. He drinks so much so quickly he suddenly gets sick and violently wretches his fill of the water he had ravaged seconds before. He rolls off his knees to sit and calm himself down and get his breath.

Still hanging on to the canteen with both hands he glances back at the dead soldiers face. This is the first Yankee he has ever seen and here he sits right beside him.

He feels the pain along his legs again so he splashes some of the water over the worst places and then pours more over his arms and hands, before taking another sip from the canteen.

Sitting there in sort of a stupor, his eyes get fixated on the dead soldiers uniform. He then looks at what is left of his own, and it aint much.

The dead soldiers coat is stained and looks soggy from the wound that must have killed him. The Union dark blue color wouldn't do anyhow he thinks. But the light blue trousers look as new as store bought, except for the dust.

Judd again examines the rags he's wearing and then his mind drifts back to the time he questioned Pa Jones about how it would be wrong to strip the dead, and Pa had said "Boy it aint stealen ifen you need it and the dead don't. Man's gotta survive best way he know how."

Judd reluctantly rises and stands over the body staring down at it. He thinks to himself "it aint right to dishonor the fallen by stealen what belongs to them" He then whispers "But, yea the word but, a useful word when it suits your purpose." He now figures in his mind "What about tonight when the chill settles in and all the tomorrows after that, if he lives so long.

He needs and could darn sure use those trousers, after all they'd just have dirt thrown on them in some old hole and be lost for ever, or be a feast for the bugs to eat them thread by thread. "I can darn sure make better use of them, by God," he says to himself.

Judd bends down and gingerly turns the body where he can unbuckle the belt. Trying as best he can to not touch the body. He tugs at the boy's shoes, figuring the trousers should come off easier with the shoes off. The body's feet are stiff already and Judd labors to remove them one by one.

The dead boy's socks are in much better shape than his own too, but he dare not and can't bring himself to take them.

Slowly he grabs the bottom of the trouser legs and pulls and yanks until at last he frees them from the body. The body's legs shine white as snow in the sunlight.

Judd carefully inspects the trousers for tears or stains and finds them to be good as new.

Judd looks over both his shoulders to see if anyone might be watching. Finding no living souls that he can see he quickly unbuttons what is left of his tattered rags and steps out of them and not wasting but a second he immediately jumps into the prized trousers.

Satisfied with the fit, his eyes again take him back to the body in search of other treasures. He decides to look inside the boy's haversack and to his delight he finds a hunk of salted bacon and a tin of crackers.

The last time he ate he reflects back must have been sometime before the morning muster and he knows he certainly hasn't had a thing since Bay Flounders death.

This day has certainly been a day to remember, he thinks to himself. He had a friend die in his arms, witnessed a battle for the first time, and might have even killed an enemy soldier. Gets himself blown up and now he's done relieved a dead boy of his belongings, eating his crackers and drinking his water. Yes this day will certainly be one to remember.

Judd throws the haversack over his shoulder, picks up the young man's musket along with his cartridge belt and stumbles off toward the sounds of battle in the distance but then stops and slowly turns around to look back at the body. He shuffles back over to the body and removes the socks and stuffs them in his pocket.

Now he is ready to face what ever is next as he walks away toward the noise and the smoke.

CHAPTER 46

In Rossville several miles to the north of the Horseshoe Ridge's Union position, General Granger stands atop a large haystack along with his Chief of staff General Isaiah Steedman. They listen to the sounds of what seems to be a raging battle taking place not to many miles to the south.

Granger's Reserve Corp officially, is in reality not much larger than a division and it has been consigned to guarding the back door to Rossville the gateway to the bridges leading to Chattanooga.

Granger has been waiting impatiently for some word from General Rosecran for the last three days.

General Granger a hard tough commander disliked by many of the soldiers he now leads is getting nastier by the second as his patience wears thin.

"Steedman, hear that racket, damn it that has to be Thomas up to his whiskers in Rebs. I want you to get down there with two brigades, Whitaker and Mitchell's.

General Steedman is naturally gifted with a lumberjack build and the courage to match. He has the respect and devotion of all the men under him, fortunately for Granger, whose situation with the men is decidedly different.

Granger, Steedman and Whitaker ride at the head of Whitaker's brigade, followed by General Mitchell and his brigade.

After marching along the LaFayette road for about an hour, Mitchell's brigade is suddenly fired on by Confederate Cavalry skirmishers patrolling the area. The attack amounts to nothing more than a nuisance, but it does slow down the brigades a bit to run them off.

To avoid further delays, Granger orders the columns to leave the road and head off through the wilderness to the southwest.

After a while when they get closer to the rear area of the Union position on Horseshoe Ridge, they begin to witness the telltale signs of a war gone wrong by the long lines of wounded men shuffling towards the safety of the low mountains to the west.

The long snaking lines of the wounded are not the only evidence of things gone wrong. The odious stench of death permeates the air that hangs low and polluted with sulfurous smog that drifts through the woods.

General Granger pulls out of the head of the column and rides back along the side of the marching men and loudly pronounces a loud warning, "men if anyone of you thinks your life is so precious as to cause you to take off and run from the enemy, be sure and realize that Company punishment won't be your share. Corporal punishment will be your fate that I promise you. There will be no cowards in this command! Run for your life you will surely lose it!"

The rear elements of the Union defenders get sight of Granger's column emerging from the wilderness and into the clearing as they approach from the rear.

The trail dust that covers their clothing fades out the color blue in their uniforms making it difficult to identify which Army they belong to.

After the close call an hour or so before, when they dealt with the dark uniforms of the South Carolina Gamecocks, the hair on the back of General Thomas's neck bristles as he waits to hear who the intruders might be.

Thomas fortunately doesn't have to wait long to calm his churning insides; Whitaker's regimental flag says it all.

General Thomas his headquarters now near the Snodgrass Field only a stones throw away from Horseshoe Ridge to his right and a similar distance to his left is Kelly Field where Generals Baird, Richard Johnson, Palmer and Reynolds have their divisions posted behind barricades along a half mile bulging front sparing against Bragg's right wing.

General Thomas receives an alarming report that a host of Confederates, maybe a division or more, are presently climbing the ridge off to the right of the 21st Ohio's flank.

Generals Granger and Steedman have just arrived and presented themselves to Thomas. Thomas hands the report to Granger to read. "General Granger," Thomas says, "your arrival at this damn time is Heaven sent. I hope your men are up for a fight, cause that is just what they are going to get."

General Granger beaming with pride to have the chance to show what his command can do remarks, "General we are ready to eat whatever the Rebs want to dish out, just show us where the table is and my troops will feed on the bastards."

Thomas amused by Grangers grit points to the west "that way General." Your seat at the table is to the right of the 21st Ohio. Whatever inspired you to come at this time is greatly I repeat greatly appreciated. Still you must hurry I'm afraid, and may God be with you Sir." With that said both Granger and Steedman salute Thomas and hurry to their horses.

CHAPTER 47

Up on the plateau where Sergeant Drake stands and oversees the construction of the latrine, Private Farr hollers from the bottom of the trench, "Sergeant you hear all that shootin? Aint it best we start getting down that way to see what's going on?"

Sergeant Drake is very aware of the sounds and in fact has been thinking of nothing else, but his orders from Lt. Simeon were explicit; get a privy dug for General Negley in a secluded area, and that is just what he will do, battle or no battle. But just the same there is some damn serious goings on back down on that ridge.

The trench isn't as deep as he would like it, "but damn it all" he says to himself, "the General will have to make do."

"Privates Drake growls, "get the hell out of that ditch and get your blouses on and form up!"

The men toss their tools aside and scramble out of the trench, quickly grabbing their coats and caps.

Sergeant Drake never has and never will chum up to the men under him. He prizes his authority and wants to keep it that way.

"Okay," he barks, "we will move and move fast. When we get back grab your muskets and get back in the line."

Private Davis, who likes to keep the sergeant stirred up says, "Sergeant what about lunch?"

Sergeant Drake steps in front of Davis nose to nose, his face flushed with anger. Davis tenses, the color fades out of his face, but he still manages a wry smile and lifts an eyebrow. Drake not foreseeing the audacity of Davis's expression has to fight off the humor he feels and digs deep to keep a stern expression. The redness in his face begins to ebb away, but he knows he can't weaken and show any sign of human emotion, so he whispers through clinched teeth, "Private your lunch was dirt today, and I sure hope you found it tasty."

Drake turns away then take a few steps and barks, "right face, at the double quick, march!"

The squad heads back down to rejoin the Company, zigzagging through the trees on the run.

Not a word is uttered, taking care to avoid a misstep on the rocky slope. But that is only part of the reason nobody is talking. Weighing heavily on their minds is what could lie ahead for them. The rattle of gunfire, the thunderous booms echoing back through the woods, leaves little doubt in their minds that they are running toward their decreed destiny.

A few wayward shots from the Confederates firing up at the Federals holding the high ground knock off some of the higher branches above them.

Sergeant Drake halts the squad for a chance to catch their breath mentions, "when we get back to the Company area I want you buzzards to keep yourselves down low. I don't want you guys losing what little brains you were born with. Then grab your rifles and get your butts back into the line. Now get some wind and we'll get moving again."

Moving as do, trotting over the gentle slope, they don't get very far when they stop again.

Down below them Drake catches sight of a large Union formation racing toward the southwest. The same direction the squad is heading.

Private Farr makes an observation, "must be reinforcements for our division. Wonder what is up?"

"I'll tell you what's up" Davis remarks, "we aint getting reinforced we're getting replaced. I'll bet a pound of bacon we get shoved right back on reserve duty again. Our dear General Thomas is gonna take care of our poor ailing General Negley, just like all Generals take care of Generals."

Sergeant Drake angry at Davis's insinuation snaps back, "well smart guy, figure this, you are as low as a pregnant sow's belly in this Army and no one gives a damn what you think. You only need to do as you are told. And I am telling you smart guy, when we arrive back to the division you will assume the duty of Company runner."

Private Farr finds this threat rather amusing that his friend has been assigned the much hated task of becoming messenger, ammo runner, and all around water boy, says, "how about that Davis I could use a little water in my canteen when you get the time."

Sergeant Drake glares over at Farr and quietly addresses him "as a matter of fact, Private you can join Private Davis and help him with his duties. So now if enough has been said we'll get moving again."

They move off a little confused by the influx of this new Union division scrambling past to the southwest.

Hurrying near the column of Colonel Mitchell's brigade, Drake's squad is unexpectedly approached by a Major riding alone, who stops and challenges them as to what they are doing and why. Since so many stragglers have been caught recently wondering off from their outfits.

"Sergeant, what is your purpose and where are you going?" the Major asked.

"Well Major Sir, we are a Detail returning to our Company." Drake remarks.

"Sergeant, what sort of Detail?"

"Latrine Detail Sir!"

The Officer has heard many a wild excuses in his short tour of duty, but Latrine Detail, is a new one. He suspects the men must be deserters from their unit. After all they are unarmed in a combat area and most likely they are unaware they are deserting in the wrong direction.

"Sergeant what division are you with?"

"General Negley's division, Colonel Sirwell's brigade, and in the78th Pa. Sir."

The Major studies the faces of Drake and the others to see if he can detect any sign of a liars flinch.

"Sergeant I find that rather hard to believe."

"Major Sir, if you would follow us to our Company area, Lt. Simeon will straighten out this misunderstanding."

"Sergeant I've got more important responsibilities at this time than to go traipsing around on a wild goose chase with you."

"Sir it isn't but a quarter mile to our line." Drake pleads.

"Your line? Sergeant I'm afraid you have made a terrible error here. I am placing you and your men under arrest. You will now come with me to the provost Officer at General Brannan's headquarters without any trouble you here.

Sergeant Drake a little angry, but worried pleads "but Sir our unit is just through the trees yonder."

"Sergeant your division pulled out and left the field several hours back. And if I had the authority I'd have General Negley arrested for desertion."

Astonished by the news an undeniable expression crosses Drakes face as he says, "How can that be? We were ordered to locate a secluded area and dig a trench for General Negley's private privy. And we did just that. When we heard all the commotion we left the ditch not so deep and headed back for our Company."

The Major for the first time can sense by Drakes eyes and voice that he is telling the truth. The Major then says, "Sergeant you and the men are free to go."

"Go, go but where Sir?"

The Major points to the south and says "There Sergeant, to the sound of the battle. The 21st Ohio can use you I'm sure. Good luck Sergeant, and to your men.

"Thank you Major Sir, I'll find the 21st."

CHAPTER 48

Major General Longstreet mounted on his horse, surrounded by his staff, observing the progress Generals Johnson and Anderson are achieving with their push to take Horseshoe Ridge.

The rumbling sound waves from the action resound back through the woods. Longstreet's attention is grabbed by a strange sound, the sound of twigs snapping in the thicket near by. He turns in his saddle and peers about, surveying the area where the sound might have come from. He is well aware Sharpshooters could very well be about, and he would make a prized target.

Finally he spots what he has been searching for and it isn't exactly what he imagined.

The sound he had heard he knew was to loud to be a squirrel, and even to loud to be that of an agile deer foraging through the woods.

Longstreet looks back over his shoulder to quietly get the attention of the First Sergeant. "Sergeant without making a fuss, look, over to your left. You'll see a solitary soldier over there stumbling around in the trees."

The Sergeant glances around in the woods, intently searching through the trees for the man.

The Sergeant whispers back, "Yes Sir I see the him, he looks to be a Yank."

Longstreet whispers back "I want you to capture him Sergeant, alive mind you, and bring him here to me."

The Sergeant removes his pistol from his holster and slowly backs his horse around. He spurs the horse and leaps away toward the man and yells, "You there halt or I'll shoot! Throw your rifle down and lift your hands high!"

The startled soldier spins around in time to see a rider racing toward him on his horse, dodging and ducking limbs and trees.

The Sergeant jumps down from his horse and quickly picks up the rifle and climbs back into the saddle. "All right you, this way," the Sergeant says as he points the way with the rifle.

The captured soldier timidly shuffles in to the clearing, his eyes wide and darting to and fro, fearing the uncertainty of what might be in store for him. He is ushered toward a group of mounted Officers. One of the Officers dismounts and awkwardly trudges toward him in thigh high boots. The rather huge man his face mostly hidden by a large slouch hat and thick bushy beard, ask the young man as he approaches "Soldier where are you bound for?"

The young man responds, "I was headen for the sounds of them guns I heard over yonder."

The Sergeant shows General Longstreet the rifle and says, "not one of our models, definitely a Union piece."

Longstreet slowly scrutinizes the young man's appearance, taking special note of the shredded remains of his shirt and scorched hairline.

"Soldier, Longstreet ask, "what is your name?"

"Judd, Judd Archer, mister."

The First Sergeant quickly protest, "Soldier that is no mister, he is to be addressed as General, and you will address him as such."

Judd steps back a step his eyes widen as he looks at the Sergeant, then at Longstreet. He can't believe, he Judd Archer is really talking to a real live General. After catching his breath he manages to say, "Sorry General Sir, I aint never seen no General before. Aint really never seen no picture of one either, excepten a picture of General George Washington on the wall at the feed store."

Longstreet can't help but grin at the naivete of his remark.

Longstreet whose responsibility it has been to send many a boy like Judd to face the uncertainty of survival against the deadly forces of war feels pity for the boy, who through his innocence has touched his heart. The General then says, "suppose you tell me what regiment you are assigned to?"

"Well yes Sir General Sir. The 44th Mississippi."

The First Sergeant not captivated with Judd, sternly ask, "and what division is the 44th with?"

"Can't rightly know Judd says "I only been in the regiment a few weeks. But my Lt. Bishop sure enough knows."

Longstreet again taken by the boys remark ask "Judd you say you are with a Mississippi regiment, how is it you are wearing Federal trousers, Federal canteen, cartridge belt and a Union rifle. Just how can that be?"

Judd kind of lowers his head, looking only at the ground and answers "Rather not say General, aint rightly proud of that. Once thought I could never do such as I did, even though Pa Jones know'd better. Pa he'd be a feller in my squad. A feller I kinda look up to that is, he being with the regiment since the start of this here war.

Longstreet wants to believe the boy, but is still puzzled how this boy got separated from his unit. He certainly couldn't or wouldn't tolerate desertion by any soldier. "So soldier how did you come by getting lost from your regiment?"

"Don't rightly know that either exactly. I know I was moving with my squad through the woods toward the Yankee line when suddenly I felt a bright hot flash cover over me that sent me tumbling. Things got awfully mixed up after that. The next thing I know'd the men had gone.

For a while I couldn't remember my name or why I was even there. I kinda walked about awhile: couldn't hear nothing, but then I started to feel some pain from the cuts and burned spots on my legs. That is when I noticed most of my trousers, was missing. But worst of all I had this real bad thirst; coulda drank up a well full of water."

Judd once again lowers his head and says, "that is when I noticed this dead Yank with a canteen. I aint much proud of what I done an all, but Satan himself must have been attempting me awful bad; I had such a terrible thirst, then I done other things I aint much proud of either.

Longstreet now really wants to comfort the boy but can't. "I see. Son I will see that you get reunited with the 44th. But first I will have an Orderly see to it that you get to a field hospital so those wounds can be dressed, and also get you a proper shirt to wear.

Longstreet ends the interrogation with a handshake and adds, "you take care son, God has truly blessed you I'd say."

The Sergeant takes hold of Judd's arm to lead him away, walking with his horse in tow, when Judd ask, "who might the General's name be?"

The Sergeant frowns, tired of this foolish inexperienced boy, says "Longstreet, General Longstreet."

Judd's startled expression says it all when he responds, "That was really him, General Longstreet?"

CHAPTER 49

Colonel Fulton's worn out brigade of Tennesseans cautiously trudge up and down the rugged terrain of hills along with Colonel Sugg's Tennessee brigade on his right.

Their orders are to out flank the Union right. The trouble is they are unable to drag their cannons with them under these conditions so they placed them on a spur of high ground several hundred yards to the rear where they can still be of use.

The climb is slow and experiences minimal harassing fire from Union stragglers sniping at them from here and there back in the woods.

General Anderson's Mississippi division is back at it again, climbing as fast as their feet will carry them. Right toward an impending storm of lead to be unleashed by the waiting 21st Ohio regiment.

Anderson's boys slowly go forth this time, depending on support from the batteries on the spur to suppress any fool enemy that dares to stand in their way. Gloriously the Mississippi banners unfurled atop their staffs as they charge headlong into a lair of death and mayhem.

Sergeant Drake with the rest of the detail, covered in dust and not very fresh form their trek, arrives at the 21st Ohio headquarter tent to report to Lt. Colonel Stoughton. At first the Colonel has no idea why these men have come to report to him.

The 21st was a part of General Negley's 2nd division, before it was sent to General Brannan's 3rd division a couple of days ago to beef up Brannan's depleted brigade after the constant combat with the damn dedicated Rebel rascals. Even so just the same, Colonel Stoughton had never laid eyes on Sergeant Drake before.

After listening to the story Sergeant Drake shared, Colonel Stoughton couldn't help but laugh.

Here in the middle of death and destruction, the story of digging a private privy for sick General Negley is a bit entertaining to Colonel Stoughton.

Sergeant Drake proud of his stripes is not amused and he is not a man to be laughed at by any man.

"Colonel you're an Officer and unless you rose through the ranks you wouldn't know about the sometime unimportant and the sometimes downright degrading duties the enlisted must carry out. Sir, me and my men are here in front of you asking to do a soldier's duty; too kill the enemy or die trying."

Colonel Stoughton also a proud man lets Drake's defiant speech pass this time, thinking he probably deserved it. Stoughton turns to his second in command Major McMahon to say, "Major find these men some equipment and assign them where they can do the most good."

As the men were leaving the headquarters, Colonel Stoughton calls out to get Drake's attention and says, "Sergeant, keep in mind some men lead and some men have to do." Sergeant Drake answers back, "yes Sir, and some men lead and do also."

Colonel Stoughton begins to rise from his stool obviously now perturbed when Sergeant Drake quickly salutes and departs figuring this might be the best time to retreat.

Major McMahon takes Drake and the rest of the new men to a supply wagon to draw them arms and ammunition.

"Sergeant take and use these well, I pray they will bring you men better luck than they did to the previous owners. He hands out the cartridge belts to Drake, who notices one of the belts has been stained by blood.

Drake peers at it for a second, then hands the clean ones to the men, saving the dirty one for his self.

The Major points to the right end of the line, "Sergeant take your men and hold that end of the line, you are now at the proverbial end of the line so to speak. By the way Sergeant, you will find Colonel Stoughton to be an excellent Officer. I hope you will be with us long enough to find that out."

Walking to their assigned position Drake has time to give it some thought at what it may take to defend the portion in the line they're responsible too hold.

He is also fully aware his men are too inexperienced. They haven't been tested enough to suit him. Only time will tell if they have the salt to stand and fight.

Drake arrives at their assigned position on the line, and first checks in with the Sergeant in charge to his left. After a few pleasantries with the Sergeant he arranges his men behind the makeshift barricade saving the far end of the line for his self. From there he can easily see a large force of Rebels in the distance making their way around to the west. Another enemy brigade is marching over the crest of a hill on a collision course with the 21st.

Drake notices Davis on his immediate left practicing lining up his sight on some phantom, like a kid playing war.

"Private Davis," Drake growls, "when those Rebs get in range, you won't have the time to take aim. You need to take the time now to learn to reload, and reload again with that five shot shooter, and damn it learn to do it quickly."

Drake stands up and addresses the others, repeating what he had said to Davis.

The Confederates to his front are closing fast and will soon be in range. The others on the far right are somewhat slower.

A dark cylindrical object arches high overhead whistling through the air and then exploding harmlessly well to the rear of the Union barricade. Soon many others follow, streaking past the 21st Ohio, slamming into the ground well behind them. The explosions create tall dark towers of soil and smoke shooting high in the air and then falling back to earth as dusty showers like dirty rain.

The Confederates coming up from the south make better time than Sergeant Drake had figured they would make.

Their throaty screams that are mixed with the detonations from the cannonade have an unnerving effect on the already exhausted soldiers, functioning mostly on adrenaline.

Sgt. Drake tries to calm his men, "keep your wits about yourselves boys, aint no one ever died from them screams. Concentrate on your duty only and when the time comes we'll start shutten em up." The little speech has the desired effect,that causes Davis's response, "Sergeant you just say when, and we'll put some lead in their yapping holes."

The others get a kick out of Davis's confidence and cheer their brother on.

The response is uplifting, but what really worries Drake, is the Rebs he sees coming from the southwest. If they ever reach a position that is perpendicular to their line, the 21st goose will be plucked.

Drake spins around to see what could be causing a ruckus he hears coming from a shallow valley several hundred yards away to the north. The sound of loud cheering sends a cold chill up his spine.

Have the Rebs somehow broken through the defenses on the north side of Horseshoe Ridge, over on Snodgrass field.

The celebrating cheers grow in intensity, as the sound moves ever closer.

Finally the tip of a staff appears, bobbing up and down on the horizon. Then emerging up as if out of the ground is the beautiful red, white and blue of the Stars and Stripes.

A mounted color guard with a Union brigade flag whipping in the wind appears at the top of the ridge.

The scene has a soothing and settling effect on Drake's raw nerves.

The sudden whistle of bullets though, zinging over his head thrust him back to the reality of the situation. The Rebels firing up the hill from the rugged draw often fire way to high. But eventually many will find their mark, and Drake knows damn well the Rebs are on their way to do what ever it takes to kill him and his Yankee brothers.

Drake pauses, takes careful aim and fires a round at some poor stranger he will never meet. And after he emptied the rest of the chambers in his revolving rifle he dismissed several other strangers he will never have to meet face to face. Quickly he reloads to continue the deadly dose to dispel other unfortunate strangers.

The Rebels keep coming like ants to sugar, and the fools are paying a high price for this pile of ground.

And now Anderson's Mississippians, with Fulton's and Sugg's Tennesseans catch more than they were expecting when General Steedman's second brigade arrives. Like a door slamming shut,

Mitchell's brigade swings in next to Colonel Whitaker's right flank, giving the Yanks more than enough men to over lap the Confederate's left by a huge margin. The superior advantage in numbers firing from the front and side is too much for the Rebels to withstand.

Not everything is all biscuits and bacon for the Yanks though. Colonel Whitaker and his entire staff are cut down, while three of Whitaker's regiments throw caution to the wind and pursue the retreating Rebels down the draw.

These brazen eager regiments, new to the contest waist no time getting over the Union ramparts and down the rugged draws looking forward to their first taste of Rebel blood.

General Steedman almost falls out of his saddle when he learns these three regiments had decided to leave the safety of the line and venture into the enemy on their own, passionately seeking the glory of it all.

To late to stop the emotional fools from their folly, they unknow-ingly hasten right into Fulton and Sugg's cannons that unleash a sheet of bolts, iron balls and jagged shrapnel into the shocked faces of the misguided Yanks, leaving scattered body parts across the ravines, along with the withering wounded unable to climb away in it's wake. The sur-vivors scratch and claw to escape the carnage in the draw.

Kershaw's Gamecocks from South Carolina seize the moment to try once again to reach the barricades on the ridge. The ground is already slick and sticky with their blood from previous attempts.

Through the chaos the smoke, shot, and the screaming wounded, one singular gallant Gamecock manages to reach the barricade where he bravely plants his battle flag he hauled up the slope, atop the rampart. His fabled act as glorious as it is, suddenly ends ingloriously when he is shot innumerable times. His flesh shredded by the multiple impacts collapses and tumbles back down the slick draw in a heap.

CHAPTER 50

Major General George Thomas has done a masterful job managing his Corp on two fronts.

His now eight undersized divisions, reduced after two and half days of fighting the relentless attacks by Polk and Longstreet. From the Viniard Field on the south end to the Kelly Field in the north, the Confederate Army under General Bragg has been repulsed time after time.

But the celebrating will have to wait Thomas is still faced with an enemy that appears to be growing in numbers, while his numbers are shrinking.

Thomas faced with this problem takes a walk to get away for a while and obviously try to sort some things out.

General James Garfield rides into Thomas's camp unexpected and is told which direction Thomas may have taken.

The two men had met many times in the past mostly at General Rosecran's headquarters so they are no strangers to each other.

Garfield sees Thomas standing off in the distance with his back to him. He rides up and dismounts. Thomas deep in thought is unaware of Garfield's presence.

"General Thomas". Thomas doesn't answer. Garfield again calls out louder, "General Thomas Sir." Thomas startled, quickly turns and recognizes the General.

"General nice to see you, have you come with General Rosecran?"
"No General, the General is in Chattanooga Sir.

"Chattanooga?" Thomas's eyes flash a questioning look.

Garfield's stare drops down as he begins to explain. "General I have come to inform you, you are to continue this campaign with full authority to due as you see fit. General Rosecran begs your pardon in this matter for he is not well at this time. You should also know our forces south of you are no longer available to support your effort here. They have all pulled back to Rossville."

"Rossville, we've got Rebs as thick as feathers on a goose on our front. How am I to be supplied?"

Garfield looks back in Thomas's eyes again and shakes his head.

Thomas then complains, "I have half my Corp posted along the Horseshoe ridge, and the other half spread out in a semicircle in the woods just a stones throw from Kelly field. The two forces are separated damn near a quarter mile from each other. My ammunition is dwindling fast and the Rebs appear to have an unlimited supply of everything.

I pray to God on most high, he'll direct me with a solution for this mess we're in. If not I just don't know."

Garfield feels for Thomas, he can see the once strapping brawny Thomas is feeling the tremendous stress from the weight of this very difficult campaign. But he can also see in Thomas's eyes a flame burning there that is far from out.

Thomas swings his arm to the east and then toward the south and says, "I can feel Longstreet's breath on the back of my neck. If I were in his shoes I'd throw everything I had into this fight and I'd do it before dark. I have to believe that is exactly what he is going to do. What I don't understand is why they have given up on us from the east. It doesn't make any sense."

Thomas pauses for minute then says, "I have to believe Longstreet is the only man directing the fight from the south. Either way I can't continue this fight for another day. I really need an evacuation plan before dark. By tomorrow we'll be out of ammunition come breakfast. Breakfast, most of my men haven't eaten since supper last."

"It is a sad day General Garfield, but that is where we stand. We are finished as an army come tomorrow, we've got the salt but not the lead to fight.

South of the Ridge, safely back in amongst the trees, Longstreet has conferred with his divisional commanders about the fortunes of war, making it perfectly clear they must attack with a unified force to be successful.

Thick smoke lies about in the deep draws and ravines, obscuring and blinding ones view to a very short distance.

Generals Manigualt and Deas troops are trying the best they can to coordinate their attack in concert with one another to corner the Union far right flank.

These two brigades try as they do, find it impossible to keep track of each other's progress under the difficult conditions.

Two Union regiments have followed their progress from the advantages of the Ridge and now position themselves appropriately to greet the Rebels with a doseage of double canister and a continuous stream of tight volleys of rifle fire.

The two southern brigades are quickly dispatched with in short order because of their failure to attack simultaneously.

The afternoon light begins to dim, and still the stubborn Yanks stand proudly at their post on Horseshoe Ridge.

General Lonsgstreet realizes deep in his soul he has no time to waist now. He must commit his reserves at once to break the hold the Federals have on the Ridge. He also feels General Polk must also get engaged immediately in his sector around Kelly Field.

General Thomas on the other side also knows deep in his soul it is only a matter of time before their time will run out. He must begin a general retreat to salvage what is left of his Corp. If only the Rebs would cooperate along the Ridge, and possibly with the beating the Rebs have taken there is a good chance they will take a break.

Thomas races on his horse across Kelly field to catch up with General Palmer to outline his plan for the evacuation of the divisions around Kelly field.

Thomas arrives at Palmer's headquarters in a flurry. The normal cordialities are swept aside, simply because he has to move quickly.

General Palmer senses the urgency when Thomas immediately goes to the map table to begin explaining how a retreat of the area will be carried out. "First General you will send a courier informing General Reynolds his division will begin the move by pulling away to the northwest using the LaFayette Road, and then turn west at the McDonald farm and proceed on through the McFarland's gap " Thomas pauses long enough to jamb a cigar between his teeth. "General you will then go next to follow Reynolds. General Johnson will follow you, and General Baird will be last to leave. All of this you understand will have to be accomplished under the Rebel noses. Palmer cuts in and says, "Fortunately they haven't been active as of late. They may however be waiting for dusk." "Or they are waiting for their reserves," Thomas adds. "Either way we'll get as many men out as we can."

"General Palmer I will depend on you to pass the word to the other commanders. Now Sir I have to figure out how to get our troops off Horseshoe Ridge. Bragg has been relentless with his attacks there all day."

"General Thomas when do we begin the evacuation?"

"As soon as you can General."

Before General Thomas could get back in the saddle, General Longstreet orders another of his reserve divisions forward to attack the Ridge once again, hoping to catch the yanks off guard or out of position. He's half right, a few of the Union regiments have been pulled back off the line because of their depleted ammunition, with the 21st Ohio equipped with their unique rifles, being one of the regiments replaced.

Nearly all the remaining Union soldiers defending the ridge are now down to a little more than a handful of cartridges. Only the arrival of Van Derveer's brigade on the left has somewhat of a supply of ammunition.

"Sergeant Drake," Private Davis speaks up while lounging with the others in the weeds trying to calm down after their frantic fight against the incessant Rebel horde.

"Sergeant I was thinking, maybe we ought to get out of here and find the 78th. We aint got no cartridges to fight with no more. So we don't have no business here anymore."

Drake looks over at Davis thinking to himself that he has come to like the lad. "Private Davis, you know you do have a knack for ideas, you do at that. But Private Davis you can't come and go as you please in this army. We have attached ourselves to the 21st Ohio for now and this is where we will stay."

Private Farr next to speak says "Sergeant why don't we go on down a ways in front of where we fought and get us some damn cartridges. I mean get some from those that aint gonna need em nomore."

"Private Farr, now that is a hell of an idea. If we get out of this alive I am going to see to it that you make Corporal."

"Oh my God," Davis exclaims, "him over us, hell I'd have to go and shoot myself in the foot before I could live with that."

"Don't make my day Private Davis, but in the mean time you and the others stay put, I've got some business to take up with the Major."

Major McMahon a stones throw away is seated upon a boulder resting with his hat in hand, notices Sergeant Drake approach, "Sergeant what can I do for you now?"

"Well Sir, I would like to ask the Major's permission to lead a patrol with my four men down the draw to procure ammunition from the dead lying about."

The Major stares at Drake for a minute, contemplating the request before saying "Sergeant you came with six men, I believe didn't you?"

"Yes Sir, two are no longer with us."

"A lot of good men are no longer with us, including the Colonel you had words with earlier. You know the Rebels may have something to say if they get you in their sights for robbing their dead."

"Well Major, I see we have but two choices, either get some ammunition, or Sir, get the hell out of here."

"Good point Sergeant, we certainly can't win with the bayonet alone, nor can you collect enough cartridges to make a difference.

No Sergeant this army needs men like you if we are to win. You are much more valuable alive, to fight the next battle, than dead for a handful of cartridges.

Drake soon discovers the Major was right, for by the time he returns to his men, all hell breaks loose once again on the Ridge.

All three of the hills that dominate Horseshoe Ridge are under attack by an exaggerated million yelling Rebs.

Like the beginning two days ago, confusion rules across the contested field of battle.

Not so as much at this time around the Kelly Field, could be the Rebs are either licking their wounds or busy preparing the way for another attack.

The evacuation plan for Kelly Field brings tremendous relief to General Joseph Reynolds, an experienced combat officer in only his early forties. A West Pointer, Reynolds is military from his epaulets to his brass buttons. But as of lately this battle has worn him thin and gotten under his skin, and sort of unraveled him. Could be the strain from being under the gun anchoring the southern flank of this Union position, although General Baird experiencing the same uncertainties at the other end of the Union position on the northern flank still has his buttons buttoned. Of course everyone is stitched a little bit differently, so our tolerances can vary. For what ever reason Reynolds is straddling crossed sabers and his constitution appears unable to handle the stress.

General Reynolds convinced his position may very well be untenable and was contemplating surrendering to the Rebel forces, when he gets the order to retreat.

He doesn't hesitate to begin orchestrating the move to get his brigades on the road. Careful not to draw attention to the move, he orders his troops to lift their feet to avoid shufflin to keep the dust from rising and forming a cloud exposing their retreat.

The Confederate aggression toward the Union defenders around the Kelly Field has slowed to a now and then artillery round and a few sporadic rifle volleys since morning.

The Southerners are still arrayed east of the Union bulge with two brigades aligned on the eastern border of the McDonald farm along the intersection of the LaFayette Road and Alexander Bridge Road just north of the northern Union flank.

General Bairds Union division posted only a few hundred yards from the before mentioned Rebel brigades under the command of Colonel Govan is closest to the Alexander Bridge Road intersection.

General Thomas needs this section of road to provide the gateway for the success of the retreat.

Inevitably the retreating brigades of Reynolds division will have to fight for this piece of property.

At first upon seeing the Rebels positioned in his way, General Reynolds loses his nerve and orders his men to throw down their arms and surrender. He now has completely folded under the pressures, much like his absentee commander, General William Rosecran.

Fortunately no one in his command is willing to listen to this insanity.

General John B. Turchin leading a brigade with three Ohio regiments and one Kentuckian approaches Govan's left flank from the woods.

General Turchin is no ordinary American General. His real name is Ivan v. Turchininoff, serving as a Colonel in the Tzars Russion Army, before migrating to New York.

He is a tenacious leader without a fearful bone in his body.

Instantly he seizes the advantage by arraying his brigade perpendicular to Govan's force without being detected and quietly orders his men to fix bayonets.

Turchin then leads the charge like a crazed Cossack, smashing into the side of the unsuspecting Rebels like a terrible blue avalanche.

Slashing and sticking his surprised foe the carnage close up and personal is too much for the Southerners, who break and scatter east through the dense forest, taking General Walthall's Mississippians along in their wake.

The road is won and is now open for the Unions evacuation plan.

General Thomas is most appreciative General Turchin had been on the spot at this most critical time. Impressed with Turchin's quick action that disperses the Confederates, Thomas wants to keep him nearby and orders Turchin to take up a position in the woods on the east side of the McDonald Farm.

Next in line to evacuate is General Palmer's division. The plan thus far is working without the slightest hint the Confederates are aware of the retreat.

That is until General Longstreet happens to request the right wing of the army to get engaged around the Kelly Field to keep the Yanks from sending reinforcements to the Horseshoe Ridge.

General Simon Buckner orders General A.P. Stewart's division to begin an attack north against the southern salient of the Union position at Kelly Field.

Stewart's brigade wary of the Union firepower moves cautiously step by step toward the Union breastworks on the southern salient. Their nerves tighten as they close, expecting a sudden volley to be unleashed in their faces at anytime. Still they move closer, inching their way until the silence is broken when they can't take it anymore and charge the enemy's barricades, yelling to release the built up tension. The roaring outcry quickly fades to a voice or two when they reach the barricade to find it deserted. Off in the distance they see the vestiges of Union soldiers moving off to the northwest.

General Palmer's division is clearing General Johnson's sector just as the Rebels begin a new assault on the Union center where Johnson is starting to initiate his pull back a regiment at a time.

The Confederates marching into Kelly Field unopposed from the south and discovering the retreat is just what General Thomas feared might happen.

All across the front the Rebels feel the adrenalin boost when they learn their comrades have gained a foothold on the enemy's southern flank. They charge forth at the once impregnable Union line with their bayonets leveled shouting their blood curdling scream. The excitement they feel to finally avenge their many dead brothers drives them on like lions at the heels of a crippled prey.

The Yanks smelled blood too, unfortunately their own this time. The debilitating fear now runs rampant through the remaining ranks along the line.

General Starkweather's once proud stalwart brigade crumbles in the face of the overwhelming Butternuts busting through their defenses.

Colonel Scribner's brigade infected with the panic on their right, unravels at the sight of Starkweather's men breaking ranks, also take off running for their lives through the swirling powder smoke, stumbling over the dead in the waning daylight.

It is every man for his self as the whole command structure is swept away by the fear of death or capture.

Many run right into the arms of the Confederates who have gained possession of the ground in the rear.

The lucky few roaming through the darkened field manage to find the portal of freedom and gather together in the forest with troops in the same boat from Horseshoe Ridge.

The last Union troops remaining on the northern tip of Kelly Field manage to evacuate before they are surrounded by the Rebs racing toward the north. The retreat though not entirely orderly is somewhat more organized in the dark than the preceding bunch in the dusk and has more success gathering with the other splintered units heading for Rossville Gap.

CHAPTER 51

A few hours before Kelly Field was silenced, men fighting for control of the Horseshoe Ridge's three hills were dying and literally coming apart at the seams.

Soldiers gathered together by circumstances now fight to live or die. Born for a purpose this was their toll for the privilege.

The proud Union boys in blue in their dusty dirty uniforms, with faces stained by the smoke of battle and streaked by sweat, so their mothers wouldn't recognize them, stood weary and worn. Their bayonets at the ready waiting for the next wave of Butternuts to try and take a piece of ground not worth spit. Short on cartridges, but long on stubborn courage, their bravery was to be tested to the limit.

A Union battery lays waste with grape shot at the Confederates trying to flank the eastern most hill, near Snodgrass Field, where the only brigade with any amount of ammunition to speak of lays a volley down that cuts the Tennessee attackers to shreds.

On the other side of the Union stronghold along the western side of the ridge the Confederates finally punch a hole in the proverbial side of the Union ship which is slowly going down with the sinking sun.

The color of the uniforms in the final light of the day makes it difficult to determine friend from foe until it is too late.

Men are captured, and some stumble around in the darkened smoke to be unknowingly blasted into eternity for their misstep.

While the blessed scramble away in the smoke and dim light, the 21st Ohio is ordered to fix bayonets and prepare to make a counter charge to liberate their old defenses.

Sergeant Drake is down right shocked by this senseless stupidity, he can't believe his ears. The audacity to suggest such a thing was asking more than he was willing to give.

He quietly gathered his men around him where he couldn't be over-heard and says, "we have been ordered back into the fight to make a bayonet charge. That's something we can't win, excepting the cheers from the Rebs. Now listen closely, we will start out, but when I give the signal we are getting the hell away, so stay close. Don't, I repeat, don't get caught up on the frenzy of the thing or you will most certainly breath your last."

"Sergeant what will be the signal?" Private Long inquires. "I don't know that now, but keep an eye on me and you will know in time." Drake responds.

Major McMahon passes by checking to make sure his men have prepared for the attack and also spreading a word of encouragement. He pauses to say a word with Sergeant Drake, "Sergeant if we are suc-cessful, you'll have your ammunition." Drake stares him straight in the eyes and says "what an awful waste Major." McMahon sighs, "you know Sergeant you'd have made one hell of an officer."

The call goes out to form up. The somber men move out without saying a word as they trudge toward the front, their only resolve was to remain brave in the eyes of their comrades.

On their way Drake concludes that if the Rebs back away he will stay, but if they try and make a fight of it, that will be his cue to leave.

Drake didn't have to wait long before the Rebels appeared out of the dense smoke like apparitions rising out of the ground from hell it self. At the same time another horde of Rebels came charging like crazed demons from the west.

The only cue Drake could come up with was "get back, get back! Stay down in the smoke and get!"

The men in the lead of the 21st were caught cold and didn't have a chance. It was either surrender of die.

The Rebs were more than willing to accommodate either way since they had to climb over the thousands of dead on their way to the top.

Privates Farr, Davis and Long have had their quest for blood more than satisfied. Their passion for war is now as distasteful as death itself, so they are more than thrilled to escape the carnage with Sergeant Drake.

They unashamedly joined many others collecting together in the woods to get free of the slaughter taking place over the entire Ridge. To be free of the suffocating stench of gunpowder smoke and death and the constant screams from the wounded is heaven sent. The trek northwest through the dark woods gives them indescribable relief for their splintered nerves. Even so they carried with them the heavy shroud of guilt in their souls for departing in defeat. However there was nothing they could have done differently, but die or languish in a prison camp. At any rate they owed their future and good fortune to Sergeant Drake. Now they must escape with the others to Rossville where they can be of use to the army yet.

Men leave the tortured woods and fields around the Chickamauga Creek, and are spared the immediate horror of it all, but many will labor with the horror they have experienced long into the sunset of their lives.

In the end the Confederate Gray have gained their prized ground and have obtained glory for their deeds at Chickamauga. Excepting of course the 35,000 casualties who will not be celebrating.

General George Thomas was the right man at the right time, with the right drive and insight to affect the soldiers lives placed in his care.

His job is only beginning with the defeat at Chickamuaga. Now he must collect the remaining survivors, disorganized and scattered in the dark on that late night and get them reorganized to restore order, confidence, and pride in themselves. He knows all too well it is only a matter of time before the Jackals will be coming to finish the kill.

On the other side time is on their side to organize, rearm, and get rested to make the final push.

FINAL CHAPTER

The following morning while Thomas works feverishly to build a formidable defense with the remains of his army, Bragg's Southerners casually go about getting their lives back together.

A Confederate ambulance wagon rolls up to an encampment on the Snodgrass farm in the early morning hours, as the soldiers are beginning to prepare their fixins for breakfast.

The wagon catches the attention of the men, stirring around their small cook fires, giving them to wonder what might be in store next.

A young man sitting next to the teamster on the wagon jumps down to the ground.

Pa Jones holding his fry pan above the flames in the fire says to Zach squatting next to him, "Well I'll be a skunk on Sunday, if that boy aint a spittin image of young Judd Archer."

Zach quickly looks over and stands up to see better, then hollers, "hey there Judd, Judd Archer over here!"

Judd's eyes light up like lanterns. He quickly hauls his gear off the wagon seat and hurries over to greet his old companions.

Pa Jones sets his pan on a rock and grabs Judd to give him a big bear hug, while Zach joyfully slaps Judd on his back and shoulders.

Pa says, "let me look at you boy, make sure you aint no ghost. I thought you done and got yourself killt yesterday morning." Judd responds, "nah, not killt, just blowed up."

Pa then says, after noticing the pants Judd is wearing, "ah, where'd you get those fancy trousers boy?"

"Same Yankee store you got yours I guess."

"Aha, you done and become a veteran now aint ya boy." Pa proudly remarks.

Before Judd could respond, Sergeant Sawyer walks up to welcome Judd back into the fold, in a Sergeants sort of way and says, "Private nice of you to finally show up, we've missed your pleasant smile around here. And to show you how much you are appreciated, when you have swallowed down your breakfast with your friends, you can take our poor water mule and fetch us some nice clean water."

Judd's mouth drops open, he can't believe his ears.

Pa quickly speaks up and says, "Sergeant Sawyer would you permit me to accompany the Private, just to make certain he doesn't get lost again?"

Mr. Jones, I think that is a fine idea. Also Mr. Jones you being such a resourceful man, I'll talk with the Company Commander about promoting you to Corporeal in the squad, that is ifin you can find me a nice pair of trousers like yours somewhere.

After a portion of fried pork Pa and Judd step off leading the horse draped with canteens that slowly swing to the rhythm of the horses lazy gait.

Pa says, "son you want to tell me about your experiences on your first battle?"

Judd a little embarrassed says, "well Pa aint much to say, excepten, you'll never guess who I had a conversation with."

So goes a moment in time, as the two side by side, fades away into the distant woods leading their horse.

CPSIA information can be obtained at www.ICGtesting.com
Printed in the USA
LVOW102149091112

306431LV00002B/13/P